A JOURNEY FOR LILY

THE RELUCTANT WAGON TRAIN BRIDE

P. CREEDEN

Sign up for my newsletter to receive information about
new releases, contests and giveaways.
http://subscribepage.com/pcreedenbooks

A JOURNEY FOR LILY

"The west is too wild for an unwed woman. If you want to ride on my wagon train and make it to Oregon, you'll need to find yourself a husband."

THE RELUCTANT WAGON TRAIN BRIDE ~ Twenty brides find themselves in a compromising situation – they have to get married in order to travel to Oregon on their wagon train. Every story in the series is a clean, standalone romance. Will the bride end up falling in love with their reluctant husband? Or will they get an annulment when they reach Oregon? Each bride has a different story ~ Read all of them and don't miss out!

When Lily Browne's father loses his job at the bank, he decides to make the journey out west, to claim land for cheap in Oregon. And when Lily hears of the need for schoolteachers out there, she decides that she must go too. There's only one problem. Even though Lily is barely nineteen, the wagon master demands that she cannot accompany the train without being wed. But she can't be a schoolteacher if she's married...

Wayne Cody became a felon by accident when

he was fifteen. After serving his time, he was released to find out that he has no family, and no more than five dollars to his name. He doesn't know much about anything other than guns, horses, and cattle, so he attempts to get hired by a wagon train to help several families make it to Oregon to claim land. If he can somehow earn enough money, he can claim land for himself, too. Then, Mr. Browne makes him an offer he can't refuse.

CHAPTER 1

April 1854

JEFFERSON CITY MISSOURI

Wayne Cody blew out a long breath and pressed the barrel of his revolver under his chin. The late April sun beat down on him from overhead and the rock he sat upon was almost too hot to bear through his dungarees. Sweat beaded on his forehead and made a trail down the side of his face before dripping off his jaw. "Oh, God," he groaned, but was unsure what else to say.

He closed his eyes, his finger moving from the guard to the trigger and then he caught himself holding his breath again. A fly buzzed around his head, and he had the fleeting thought that the fly was likely to eat well soon. That brought other morbid thoughts to mind about maggots and other creatures that might find his body once he pulled the trigger. But when would a human find him?

He sat outside the limits of the town of Jefferson City, not too far off the main roadway, but other than the road, there wasn't much more than stretches of barren wilderness in all directions. It might be a few days before someone would wander off the trail far enough to find him. Would the livery keeper look for him when the horse Wayne had bought for three dollars showed back up at the livery? He doubted it.

Another breath expelled from his lungs; another droplet of sweat made a trail down the side of his face. A horse whinnied in the distance, causing the one whose reins he held to wicker softly in return. Would the person see his horse? Perhaps if Wayne waited just a bit longer, his gunshot would catch the attention of the traveler heading his direction. Then maybe he'd save himself from being eaten by whatever creature took a fancy to his carcass.

That made him huff a small laugh even though it wasn't funny. His heart rate had slowed. How long was he going to sit there before pulling the trigger? The steel in his palm was heating up from the sun blazing upon the rest of the gun. Maybe he should just pull the thing away, at least until the rider came closer. Somehow the thought of doing that made him feel weaker, more cowardly.

Or was he taking the coward's way out already?

Maybe. But would it really be brave at all to keep on living in a world where he had no one—not one family member to speak of? Not one friend. No job prospects, as a felon. And hardly more than a dollar to his name now that he'd spent three on a horse?

If only.

If only he hadn't drunk that whiskey on that day when he was fifteen. If only he hadn't gone along with it when Joe and Bill had decided to go turkey shooting after they'd been drinking. If only Bill hadn't let off a shot too close to the Reed's home. If only that bullet hadn't hit Mrs. Reed and injured her gravely. If only Mrs. Reed hadn't died before the trial started. If only those two brothers hadn't pointed the finger at him.

Then, maybe he would have been at home helping his mother around the farm so that she hadn't died two years before the end of his ten-year sentence. And prison had been hard on him. There were people who called the Missouri Penitentiary the bloodiest acres in the state. And they wouldn't be wrong. Only the strongest men survived. The weaker men ended up dead or enslaved in manners unbefitting to mention. Wayne had had to fight so that he wouldn't end up in one of those two conditions. Back then he'd fought for his life, but he'd paid for it in other ways. He'd lost a molar on the left side in one fight, ended up with a scar across his right cheek that had healed a bright shade of pink and caused that part of his face to sink in a little bit. And his now crooked nose had been broken three times. Getting employment had become impossible for him. With just a look at him, he was turned away before he could get one word out of his mouth.

"Oh, Lord, I'm sorry..." he groaned again.

The world would be better off without him. Living in the prison had been hell enough, surely the hell that was saved for people like him who took their own lives couldn't be any worse. A tear welled in his eye and slipped out from under his lid, joining the sweat trails to his chin. Or maybe God would have mercy on him since he'd only been in that situation because of an accident and an accusation, even though he'd been innocent the whole time.

Not that anyone believed him.

His shoulders slumped. And he could just about hear the hoof beats behind him. Time was up. He needed to go ahead and get this over with before he lost his resolve. Sitting up straighter, he took a deep breath and held it for half a moment, preparing to pull the trigger on his exhale.

"Cody? Is that you?" a familiar voice called out from behind him.

Confusion and embarrassment both struck Wayne in equal measures as his eyes snapped open. He yanked the revolver from his chin and stood quickly, wiping his face on his sleeve before spinning on his heel. He swiped at his face once more hoping there'd be no trace of his tears.

Sitting upon a chestnut mare, Mason Bradley offered a gap-toothed grin and pushed his straw hat up a little off his forehead. "I thought that was you. Didn't you leave the pen three days ago? I thought you'd be long gone by now."

Clearing his dry throat, Wayne looked down, dusting off his dungarees in a moment to gain composure. Then he shook his head. "Got no where to go."

Bradley's brow lifted. "Really? No where?"

A lump formed in Wayne's throat, and he shook his head.

"Why don't you come with me then? I'm heading up to Independence. My uncle there is a supplier of cattle and oxen for fools trying to make it on the trail to Oregon. It's easy money and he's always hiring a cowboy or two. I'll put in a good word for you."

Wayne blinked at the man and swallowed hard. "Why would you do that?"

Bradley shrugged. "I just thought with a mug like yours, even the railroad wouldn't hire you. Call it pity if you want." He sat up straighter in the saddle and reined his horse back to the road. "If you don't want to come, then don't come," he called out from behind him as he started trotting away.

His heart suddenly racing, Wayne pulled the bay gelding he'd bought by the rein to draw him closer and then shoved his foot into the stirrup and mounted while the horse had already started away at a trot after his buddy from the livery. Wayne barely managed to right himself in the saddle and shove his felt hat upon his head before catching up to Bradley.

Bradley eyed him with a half-cocked grin and nodded. "Ain't you glad that you helped me out that one time in the yard?"

Even though he nodded, Wayne's brows scrunched as he tried to remember. He and Bradley had always been on friendly terms with each other, but never quite friends. And Wayne didn't remember helping the man out, but it didn't mean that he hadn't in some manner. Fights were frequent in the yard, and sometimes he'd just find himself involved.

Regardless, as they rode their horses toward the northwest, Wayne sent up a small silent prayer. It wasn't much more than just a thanks. But he hoped that God, at least, knew what he meant.

LILY BROWNE SQUINTED OVER HER SPECTACLES OUT the window of the Independence hotel, trying to make out the shapes of the men on the street. Her father had worn his smart, gray suit and she had hoped to make him out by the color. Her spectacles helped her to read and to make out faces when they were close, but even her vision farther away seemed to be getting worse. She didn't want to bother her father with that small thing now, so she decided to live with it until they made their way out to the west.

A small cough came from the bed next to the

window, and Lily turned toward the sound. Her nine-year-old brother, Thomas, sat up from the bed slowly, his pallor making his eyes seem an impossible shade of blue. She scrunched her brows as she stood, setting her book and spectacles on the table before she came over, resting a hand upon his forehead to see if he was feverish.

"Do you think I could go outside today?" His eyes met hers, and his voice sounded a bit dry.

She reached for the pitcher by the table and poured him a glass of water. "If you're feeling strong, we could go down to the dining room and get you a bite of something to eat. And if you're still up for it, we can take a short walk along the street."

A broad smile spread across his lips as he threw aside his covers and took the glass from her. He took a quick sip and tried to return it to her hands.

She shook her head and pushed the glass back toward him. "Drink it all, please. It will make your throat feel better."

He huffed, but did as he was asked and downed the whole glass. This time, though instead of handing it back to her, he set it down on the table with a clink. "There. Now can I go get ready?"

"Of course," she said with a smile and stepped back toward the window to give her brother some privacy while he changed behind the screen. Again, she picked up the spectacles and looked through and over them a few more times, trying to determine which method to use when trying to see farther away. Finally, she decided that she could see better without the spectacles when trying to see as far as the street. Her brother shuffled behind her. He'd lost so much weight, his clothes were at least a size or two too big now. The sickness had taken away his appetite and how could her brother heal if he didn't eat well? Even though her father talked almost constantly about the adventures they'd be having in this trip across the Wild West, she knew their reason for going was two-fold. So that her father could gain land and employment, and so that her brother could get the air that he needed to get better.

"I'm ready," Thomas finally called out with a voice that was more chipper than she'd heard in the last few days.

"Okay," Lily said as she turned around, "but I want to see you eat at least half your eggs before I even think about letting you go for that walk. And a few bites of toast and oatmeal too."

Her brother groaned but nodded his head. "As long as I can go for a walk outside, I'll eat twice that much."

A smile pulled on Lilly's lip. She'd love to see him eat as much as he said. Together the two of them started out the door of their room and down the hallway to the stairs. If her brother could make it down the flight of stairs to the dining room without having to catch his breath, Lily would count that as a blessing all in itself.

CHAPTER 2

End of April 1854

INDEPENDENCE

Mason Bradley had kept his word and made sure that Wayne got employment with the cattleman who supplied beef to those making the trek out west along the trail. The country in this part of Missouri was much more serene than it had been at the penitentiary. Even though the Main Street area of Independence was cluttered and noisy, out in the cattle fields and by the river, an overwhelming sense of peace came over Wayne. He sat upon his bay gelding as it drank some of the water from a slow-moving stream, listening to the low mooing of the cattle as they picked at the grass on the hills just above him. Once his horse finished drinking, Wayne reined him back up the hill to join the other two cowboys who were still watching the herd.

"Pa says it's a racket, so I wish I had the kind of money it takes to sell cattle and oxen and such to these crazy people who are going on the trail," one of the cowboys, Garrett was his name, said.

"Why are they crazy?" Josiah, the other cowboy asked as he tipped back his tan hat off his forehead.

Wayne frowned. He was the eldest of the three cowboys—who were only teenagers—so wasn't sure he even wanted to get involved in their conversation, but he wanted to stand in the shade under the tree with them to avoid the heat of the day so he settled in, trying not to listen too hard.

"My Pa says that as many as go on the trail to get land or gold or whatever reason, that almost a third of them don't make it. Die of sickness, accidents, snakebites, get caught in the snow, or even Injuns," he said that last bit in a harsh whisper, looking around as though one might pop out of the brush after hearing him summon them. "Besides, these crazy people seem to have more money than sense. Pa says that they pay almost three times as much for the cattle as the stockmen get them at the auctions.

Only Mr. Bradley sells them at a reasonable price, and Pa says he's a fool for doing so."

Wayne frowned and cleared his throat. "Honesty doesn't make a man a fool," he said, unable to let it slide. Then he reined his gelding to the west where he saw one of the steers heading away from the herd. Without much work, he guided the young steer back toward the rest of the cattle. One of the things he liked about Mr. Bradley, Mason's uncle, when Wayne had first met the man, was that he immediately invited them both to dinner with them. Mr. Bradley had said grace over the meal, and read scriptures afterward. Word had gotten around among the cowboys that no one should cuss or tell a colorful joke around him as he was a churchgoing man. Wayne had met many men who went to the saloon on Saturday and then got up for church on Sunday. But Mr. Bradley wasn't that kind. He seemed to live what he read in those pages.

Though they had a pastor come out to the penitentiary on Sundays, and had bibles there for the men to read, it didn't help much because most of them couldn't. There was an older prisoner by the name of Shacklesford who would read the scriptures aloud, similar to the way that Mr. Bradley did, but he kind of just did that in the most annoying way possible to most of the folks in the prison. Shackles-ford would read aloud during mealtime and for a couple hours in the evening while each man was locked up in their cell. Some of the men took to yelling blasphemies at the man, and telling him to "shut up," but Shacklesford kept on reading, and people didn't mess with him for it. It was almost like he was considered a kind of holy man.

Wayne would listen to the man reading the word, lying back in his cell and imagining the stories and what it was like to be one of those bible men. They seemed more relatable than he'd realized. The preachers never talked about how even the men that God chose to do his work seemed to be weak or make mistakes, just like everyone else did. Wayne had never realized before that God didn't always choose the most powerful, most wordy, or smartest. He seemed to pick just normal men to do what he needed done.

Even as he sat on his horse, Wayne let out a sigh. He'd almost went and met his maker the other day when he thought all was lost. Now he was over a hundred miles away from the prison and working in a field with a belly that wasn't grumbling at him. Apparently the word was right when it said that God's ways were not the same as his own ways.

Maybe he just needed to trust the plans that the maker had for him.

In the distance, he heard the sound of a cowbell ringing mightily, and three cowboys were making their way out toward them, the one at the front was Mason Bradley, himself. Wayne couldn't help but crack a smile as he stretched his back and stood in the stirrups a moment to give his seat a bit of a break. The men rode straight for him, and the two teenagers that were behind Wayne also rode over at about the same time.

Mason nodded and offered a smile. "Y'all ready for a night in a bed instead of sleeping out here in the field?"

"Ha!" Josiah shouted. "I'll be happy just to get a full night's sleep instead of having to take a watch."

"That's for sure," said the other teenager.

Mason doffed his hat and waved it in the direction of the bunkhouse. "Then off y'all go."

The two boys took off like a race had been called and the starting shot had been fired. The bay gelding under Wayne immediately started jigging and chomping at the bit. His front end getting light as he offered to rear from being held back. He nodded his thanks in Mason's direction and then gave the gelding his head. Immediately the horse leapt forward, causing Wayne to grab the horn and brace against the sudden forward lurch. Then Wayne leaned forward, letting the gelding's powerful legs move under them, each one pumping hard as they made their way in the same direction as the two boys' horses. Being just a livery horse, the gelding had no chance of catching the other two cow ponies, but Wayne was willing to let him try.

When they made it to the gate just a couple minutes after the two boys, the horse finally slowed, its sides heaving as it huffed and puffed. Garret had opened the gate from atop his horse and was letting both Josiah and Wayne through. Though the two cow ponies didn't seem quite as out of breath as his livery horse, they had just as much foam and sweat forming on their chests as he imagined his own gelding did. Once through the gate, the boys trotted their way down the lane. They were local boys, apparently, with family in town or nearby. They wouldn't be staying in the bunkhouse for their reprieve the way that Wayne would. Ever since the last auction, when they'd brought in almost a thousand head of cattle, the cowboys were watching the stock both day and night to make sure that no one touched them—thief or predator. Each group of three kept watch for three days and then got a reprieve for three. That way no one got too tired and ended up falling asleep when it was his watch.

Even though being stuck with the conversation of two teens for company could be a bit tiring at times for Wayne, he preferred their innocence to what he'd experienced the last decade while he'd been imprisoned. By the time he was their age, he'd already been serving a year or so of his sentence. What would it have been like to be raised like one of them? He shook his head. It wasn't like he could go back in time and change what had happened. It was better that he just live his life the best he could with what he had now.

He was heading for the bunkhouse when he remembered that the cook was one of the three cowboys who'd relieved them from the field. With a groan, Wayne slumped his shoulders and reined his horse toward the front gate, following after the kids who'd just left the ranch for town. Only this time, he'd be going at his own pace rather than allowing his horse or those teenagers to decide his pace for him.

"FAMILY HUG!" THOMAS, LILY'S BROTHER SAID AS HE gripped both Lily and his father in a hug that included all three of them.

They squeezed each other tightly for a moment, then Mr. Browne, Lily's father rubbed the top of Thomas's head. "Off to bed with you now. Good night."

"Good night," Thomas said as he climbed over the footboard of the hotel bed and lay down.

For the next twenty minutes, Lily's father paced across the hotel suite mumbling to himself. For a long while, she just watched him moving back and forth in front of the bedroom door, wondering if he might wear a groove in the wooden floor. She sat upon the bed with her younger brother, gently stroking Thomas's back, to lull the child off to sleep. Once she felt the gentle rise and fall of even, sleeping breaths, she made her way out of the room and into the suite area with her father. "Penny for your thoughts?" she offered.

He stopped in his tracks and huffed a sigh. Twice, he started to speak, only to stop himself and shake his head. For a moment, Lily wondered if he might start pacing again. Then he met eyes with her, and she saw the sadness there. "I'm not sure how we're going to do it."

She tilted her head in question. "What do you mean?"

Standing akimbo, he shook his head, casting a glance at the floor again. He lowered his voice and leaned into her. "I don't think your brother will make it with our current arrangements."

The statement made Lily's heart sink, and she understood finally why there was sadness in her father's eyes. A lump formed in her throat, and she had to swallow it down in order to speak. She whispered again, "What do you mean?"

"It's a long journey, Lily. It might take us as little as five months on the trail, God willing, but it might take six...or more. And to ask him to sit upright on the seat of the wagon for the entire trip while you and I walk beside the oxen with all of our belongings in the back of the cart. It just doesn't seem right."

A frown tugged at Lily's lip. "So, what should we do?"

"That's exactly what I've been trying to figure out. I'm not sure we can leave things behind in order to make room for Thomas in the back. We'd want a significant amount of room and we've already parted with so many things when we left Virginia. I don't want to go back through them again and decide what else should go."

Lily nodded. That wasn't something that she'd want to do either, but if they needed to for Thomas, she knew that they both would be willing.

"So, the only thing that makes logical sense is for us to buy a mule team and a second wagon."

She blinked. "What?"

"The second wagon could be smaller, so we could have a mule or two pull it instead of a team of oxen. But it would mean that you'd have to drive the wagon yourself so that you can keep care for your brother. You're an accomplished horsewoman, so I know you could handle the reins. But I'd hate for us to be split up most of the day like this. However it would give us a covered wagon that might be possible for you to share with your brother when we bed down at night. It gives me peace of mind to know that you'd both be safer than if you're laying in the dirt like most others who'd be traveling the trail."

She felt cold as the blood drained from her extremities. "You'd want us to handle two wagons with all of our supplies and such—just you and me."

Suddenly, he rubbed the back of his neck and looked down sheepishly. "Actually, it's not going to be just you and me. We're joining a wagon train."

A sense of relief washed over her, and her cheeks felt hot as the blood returned to her face.

But that moment was short lived as soon as her father finished taking another breath. "But there's only one stipulation to us joining the train. The wagon master has a strong feeling that he wants an environment of safety and security for everyone in his train. Therefore he doesn't allow any unwed women of marrying age to join the train and drive on their own."

Her frown returned and she shook her head. She was nineteen years old. In Virginia, sixteen was considered a reasonable age to get married, but she'd gotten an education instead. For a while she wasn't sure if she wanted to study nursing or become a teacher. She'd chosen the latter, but when her brother grew ill, she wished she'd studied nursing instead. Regardless, when her father had decided to move to Oregon and claim land there, Lily had discovered the demand for teachers out that way was great and made up her mind to come along and help. "But... I must remain single in order to teach. They don't allow married women to become school-teachers." Her voice cracked when she spoke, and she was unable to look her father in the eyes.

Her father's gaze held hers and remained steady

as he placed a gentle hand upon her shoulder. "Do you trust me, Lily?"

Lily clenched her teeth, feeling uncertainty welling in her stomach, but she nodded.

"I will take care of it. I promise you that you will have nothing to worry about. Okay?"

She nodded again, feeling tears sting the backs of her eyes as that lump rose in her throat again. Yes. Of course, she trusted her father, but wasn't this too much to ask? How could he possibly keep her from having to be wed if the wagon master decreed it compulsory in order to be part of the train? Without question they would be safer traveling with a train and there might even be a cook and some extra stock of supplies so there would be less to worry about while they travelled. Still, Lily couldn't help but worry about what solution her father had in mind and if it would really work.

CHAPTER 3

Having just finished dinner at the local saloon, Wayne decided to walk through town a bit and stretch his legs. The sun hadn't quite set yet and was casting a golden glow over the town of Independence, making it feel almost heavenly. Maybe it was his full stomach and the satisfaction he had for the work he'd been doing, but this little walk was really making him feel satisfied with his life for the first time in over a decade. For the last three days he'd rarely gotten out of the saddle, and even when he did, he didn't get much of a chance to walk around. It was either work the cattle or sleep on his bedroll. There wasn't much more to it than that. The heels of his boots clacked across the wooden boards that lined the porches of the saloon and the barber shop that sat next to it. Then he took a step down into the dust and dirt, strode forward three times across the alley and stepped up onto the next board-walk that ran in front of the general store.

The shops hadn't quite closed yet, so there were people milling about and he'd had to walk sideways for a moment to avoid a pretty young lady that was leaving the store. The young blonde smiled up at him briefly, her blue eyes sparkling, and Wayne's heart skipped a beat. Women didn't usually look up at him and smile. They usually avoided his gaze and hurried away from him. He knew that the scar on his face made him look like a ruffian, so he couldn't blame them. "Good evening," he managed to say.

"Good evening," she said back, her gaze not faltering and her smile undeterred. Then she finally broke her gaze and started away.

How could such a pretty girl as her not flinch away from him? He watched as she made her way down the boardwalk toward the inn, still in awe. The sight of her and the way that she didn't change made him chuckle. Things finally seemed to be going right for him for once in his life and he felt giddy about it. Someone might even think that he'd been drinking to put him in this mood, but he'd never had a sip of the stuff. His father had been a drunk and a gambler, and Wayne had decided a long time ago that he wasn't going to follow in his father's footsteps. He stepped off of the boardwalk again and shot another glance over toward the hotel. Perhaps he could afford to get a room and sleep in a fancy bed for the night. Maybe he'd even catch sight of that pretty young girl again. The thought flitted through his mind, but he immediately brushed it all away. He'd never want the girl to become uncomfortable, thinking he'd followed her.

And besides, he had a cot waiting for him in the bunkhouse, which he'd be sleeping in alone—so no snoring from others to deal with. It wasn't the time to get greedy just to sleep on a featherbed with scented sheets. Though he might have the two dollars needed to stay the night there, it wasn't how he should spend it—he knew that much. Still, he had to admit that the temptation pulled at his heart just a little. Instead, he made his way across the street to the livery where he'd left his horse to graze in a paddock while he'd gotten his own dinner at the saloon.

"That can't be right. You want eighteen dollars for each mule?" A man standing in front of the livery asked. "I paid you nearly fifty for my oxen; can't you cut me a better deal? I don't have a lot of money to spare but I really need those mules."

"You had enough money to buy a second cart. Seems to me that if you have that many things that you're taking with you to Oregon, you can afford a little more for a mule. It's a good pair of jennies. They drive well and go right along with little coaxing," the livery owner said, his thumbs in his belt loops as he peered down at the shorter man in a brown suit.

The man shook his head and cast a glance downward.

Wayne frowned as he drew closer to them. He recognized the older gentleman in the spectacles. The man had been in the saloon and was the only other person in the bar who wasn't drinking alcohol along with Wayne. It had been strange that the man had been people watching in such a brazen way. Wayne could tell that he was making other people, especially the bartender, nervous. Eventually the man left as though he was disappointed. But right now, the man was right. He was being price gouged, and a prick of injustice tugged at Wayne's heart. He cleared his throat, causing both men to look his direction. He didn't miss the man's look of desperation as they met eyes. Feeling a bit more brazen,

Wayne stood taller. "Don't you think that you should give the man a discount since he's already given you enough to pay for both the oxen and the mule. If he went to another town, we all know he'd pay much less for a jenny like that."

The livery man's gaze turned into a glare as his face reddened. He threw up a hand in exasperation. "Then let the man go to the next town. I'm giving him a fair, Independence price for both oxen and mules. These animals are in high demand and they don't come cheap. If he doesn't buy the mule, I'll just sell it to the next man. And who are you to stick your nose in my business?"

And with that, the livery man turned on his heel and started walking away, dusting off his palms as though he was finished with the conversation. The man in the suit cried out. "Wait, wait! I need those mules. I can't pay the full amount right now, but I'll find a way."

The man in the suit took a step toward the livery man, but Wayne couldn't stand it any longer. He reached out and took the man by the upper arm. "Wait, sir. You don't need to demoralize yourself to suit a man who is trying to take you for more than a mule is worth. I know a man who can provide you them at a reasonable price."

Wide eyes looked into Wayne's as though trying to judge whether he should believe. This gentleman seemed to be distraught and desperate. Some people would try to take advantage of a man in such a situation, and Wayne knew that it was not a good man who would. His feelings on the matter were justified.

He nodded in reassurance to the man. "I'll take you there right now if you'd like."

Slowly the man's unbelieving eyes filled with gratitude. "Yes. Thank you."

ON THE WAY TO CHURCH THE NEXT DAY, LILY'S FATHER held her younger brother in his arms, carrying him instead of allowing him to walk. They wanted to be sure that he'd have the energy to sit in a pew for an hour or longer if the sermon carried on. But still, her father couldn't help but talk in excited tones about what had occurred the night before. "Then the young cowboy took me to a ranch. I wasn't sure at first, since it seemed to be mostly cattle that was sold there, but apparently they sold more. I was provided with a first rate pair of mules, even bigger than the ones that I was going to get at the livery for nearly half of the price."

Lilly smiled and nodded. "You'll have to thank that gentleman when you see him again."

"I don't know if I will see him," her father said with a bit of disappointment in his voice. "He seemed a pretty rough fellow and didn't appear to get off the ranch very often. It was fortuitous that he came along right when he did. I would never have taken the cowboy to be such a gentle soul when I'd seen him in the saloon just before. But now that I recall, I don't believe he'd been at the bar getting spirits. I believe he was just taking his supper there."

"That's good. It also seems to be right for a gentlemanly type to not be there carousing," Lily said as they reached the steps of the white chapel.

"Well," her father said as he set Thomas down and gave the boy a pat on the head. "A true gentleman wouldn't take his dinner in a saloon, either if he could help it. But we don't know what everyone's situation is or how hard their lives might be, so it's best to give a man the benefit of the doubt in those circumstances and not judge them."

Again, Lily nodded and held her brother's hand as they made their way up the steps to sit in a pew. It wasn't long before the organ at the front of the building began to play and the benches were filled with people of all kinds wearing their Sunday best.

The songs were solemn and called sinners to repentance while the sermon itself was delivered with heart and emotion. When Thomas grew tired toward the end, he lay curled up on the bench with his head in Lily's lap. In her heart, she hoped that others might take the same thought to mind as her father had expressed moments before and not judge him for lying down in church, or her for not being able to stand to sing the final hymn.

When they reached the end of the service, Lily helped her brother up. People around them all introduced themselves or said hello to Lily's father, if they'd met the week before. The Browne family had been in Independence for a little over two weeks making preparations for their journey, and now that they were joining a wagon train, something stirred in Lily's stomach akin to fear. Yes, it was exciting to think on the prospect of finally getting started with the journey, but she feared what they might encounter. She wasn't a child any longer, so she knew the trip wasn't going to be all sunshine and roses. Some called the journey treacherous. Some said it was deadly. Regardless, there were many willing to make the journey as though there were a pot of gold waiting for them all in the end.

There may not have been gold waiting for Lily in

Oregon, but if the trip could help her brother's health and give him a longer life, it would be worth the journey. And it would give her an opportunity to help more children like him in getting an education out west as well. And those prospects turned the churning in her stomach to something more like butterflies. That relief made it better.

"Lily, I see someone I'd like to speak to. Would you mind taking your brother back to the hotel?" Her father asked and then kneeled down to Thomas's height. "Do you think you have the strength to make it on your own."

Thomas nodded, holding his arm up and flexing it as though he were muscular. "Yes, Father. I have the strength of an ox." To prove it, he pulled both Lily and their father into a squeezing embrace. "Family hug!" He declared, his voice muffled by the way his face was stuffed into them. They chuckled as they were released.

Then Father tilted his head and lifted a brow, but a smile tugged at the side of his mustache-covered lip. "All right then. I'll trust you to make sure that your sister arrives safely?"

"You can count upon me, Father." Thomas grabbed hold of Lily's hand with more strength than she knew he could muster and started for the door to the church.

Lily couldn't help but let another chuckle bubble up. It was good to see her brother in such high spirits, even though the same old fear made its way to the back of her mind. How long would this strength last? Would they make it all the way back to the hotel without Thomas needing a rest?

Her brother coughed, covering his mouth with his free hand, and that fear within her intensified. But his hold upon her hand never wavered as he led her down the steps of the chapel and started down the street toward the inn. She'd have to trust him, and in the meantime, keep up the pace since he'd set off at a fast lick. It made Lily hopeful that he'd make it all the way back strong, even if he then had to lie down once they arrived.

Although his pace slowed, they managed to make it back to the inn. Lily eyed her brother as they entered the shade of the foyer. Sweat trickled down both sides of his face and some of his dark blond hair stuck to his temples. But his eyes were determined as he started directly for the stairway. Finally, Lily pulled upon his hand. "Wait."

He stopped and looked at her fully, his breathing labored, but not raspy. "What is it?"

She swallowed and fanned herself. "I'm just so tired after the walk," she said, looking for some kind of excuse that he'd accept. "Let us sit down here in the parlor, for just a moment, before making our way up the stairs?"

His shoulders drooped a bit and a disappointed wrinkle furrowed between his brows. "Are you sure? It's not very much farther to walk, you know."

She nodded. "I know, but I just need a short rest, all right?"

A sigh escaped his lips. "Fine. Let's sit a moment."

For a long while they both sat upon the red velvet loveseat that was at the bottom of the steps and to the left. Lily continued to keep an eye on her brother from the side, trying not to be too obvious. Even her young brother had a sense of pride. She knew it was what drove him to march all the way back from the church to the point where he now breathed heavily.

Thomas wiped the sweat from his brow.

She was already feeling a bit cooler after a few minutes, so she knew that Thomas would be too. His breathing had become more even, but she still wanted to give them both a minute more before braving the stairway. She leaned forward. "I'll be back momentarily."

He frowned. "What is it now?"

"I'm thirsty," she answered. "I'll get us both a quick glass of lemonade from the dining room.

Shaking his head, Thomas deepened his frown. "I don't need it."

Standing, Lily shook her head back at him and lifted her chin. "Well, I do," she said and left him sitting on the seat while she headed toward the dining area.

Quickly she ordered both glasses and paid for them at the cashier. All the while, she kept peeking around the corner at her brother to make sure that he remained where she left him. With a smile, she accepted the two glasses from the waitress and then walked back into the parlor with them and handed one to her brother.

Even though Thomas had said he didn't want one, he took it and licked his lips before taking a solid gulp. With a smile, Lily sipped at hers, savoring both the tartness and the sweetness. She'd only drank half by the time her brother had downed his entire glass. She lifted a brow at him as he took a deep breath, obviously feeling much better. The refreshing drinks had done exactly what she'd hoped. Her brother was breathing better, the coolness had helped alleviate his heat, and the sugary sweetness had given him what appeared to be an infusion of energy. He swiveled his head toward her and smiled. "Are you ready?"

She set her glass down beside his on the side table, knowing the waitress would be by later to retrieve the glasses. Then she nodded. "I believe so."

When her brother offered his hand again, she took it and the two of them made their way up the stairs. Perhaps she and her father were babying him a bit too much. Maybe he was stronger than they assumed. Either way, she was happy that he seemed to be making it to the hotel on his own without a problem and with few coughs. Perhaps they'd overcome this bout with illness yet.

CHAPTER 4

Hat in his hands, Wayne frowned as he looked down at Mr. Bradley's boots. They stood outside the gate of the ranch together, having let the other cowboys who'd attended church with them go on, until the two of them were left alone there at the gate. His boss, Mr. Bradley set a hand on Wayne's shoulder. "This isn't the way that I would have it, myself, son. But I have to keep the peace in town. I can't be having our ranch and the livery at odds with each other. Mr. Miller at the livery demands that I make amends for the loss that you caused him yesterday. If I'd known the full story, I wouldn't have sold that man you brought here those mules at all."

With that, Wayne looked up, meeting his boss's

eyes. "But sir, Mr. Miller was price gouging the man. It wasn't fair."

Mr. Bradley's eyes were soft with understanding, but his frown remained. "Unfortunately, there are many men in town who take advantage of those who are making their way on the trail. Not everyone is going to give a fair price. But the truth is that I will likely never see that man, Mr. Browne, again, but I will have to make deals with Mr. Miller for years, perhaps decades, to come. So, I need to stay out of that business, do you understand?"

He didn't like it, but Wayne nodded.

"So, will you go down to the livery and apologize, and give him the money that we made off the mules, so that we can make amends."

Wayne's stomach churned at the thought. "But I did nothing wrong—and I need to apologize?"

Mr. Bradley's face remained solemn as he nodded. "I'm afraid so."

Squeezing his hat tighter in his grip, Wayne clenched his teeth at the injustice. He'd have to apologize to a man who he'd done nothing wrong to. Wayne had already spent a decade in prison serving time for a crime that he didn't even commit. It was unfair. It was wrong. Why did fate always deal him a bad hand of cards? He couldn't see the reason in it. Inside he broiled, and his face heated.

After a moment, Mr. Bradley squeezed the shoulder he still had his hand upon. "You'll do it, won't you, son?"

Honestly, Wayne didn't know if he could. He'd have to eat humble pie and not only apologize to someone when he had done nothing wrong, but that someone was the one who'd actually done the wrong. It would be like apologizing to the two brothers who'd landed him in prison in the first place for their own wrongdoing. He'd be a laughing-stock, wouldn't he? Slowly he shook his head. "I don't think I can."

A disappointed sigh released from Mr. Bradley's lips as he withdrew his hand, forcing Wayne to look back up at his boss as the man said, "Then I don't know if I can continue to offer you employment here."

Grief, like a bucket of cold water dumped upon Wayne's head overcame him. His blood froze like ice in his veins. He felt betrayed once more by a man he'd trusted. A good, Christian man. How could a man like Mr. Bradley do this to him? How could God do this to him? "You'll let me go because I can't apol-ogize for something when I did no wrong?"

Mr. Bradley released another sigh before he said, "Son, the world is wrong. It's been broken since Adam and Eve ate that fruit in the garden of Eden. Sometimes we get good things that we don't deserve, like God's grace. And other times, we get bad things when we don't deserve them either, and this is one of those times. Consider for a moment what would happen if you stand your ground and don't apologize, but continue working here at the ranch. Mr. Miller will always hold a grudge. He'll make all the deals that the ranch has with him sour with his resentment. He'll look on me... you... and other Christians who are witnessing to him as though we think that we're better than him. He'll be goading us on and waiting for us to fail and spitting upon God's calling for his life. But if you do the right thing, if you apologize, then he'll let this whole thing go. Sure, he might gloat a bit and hold it over you for a short while, but after that, life will go on. He'll forget, lose his anger and resentment, and be more open to the calling of Christ."

A lump had formed in Wayne's throat and the bitterness he'd had a moment before had receded. He could understand what Mr. Bradley said with his mind, but still his hands gripped his hat and that betrayal still stung in his heart a little. He shook his head again. "I just don't think I can do it, sir."

"I understand." Mr. Bradley patted Wayne on the shoulder and then he pulled out a small, worn Bible from his pocket. "Wayne, I know this is a difficult situation, and I can't make the decision for you. But remember, we're called to be peacemakers and to show love, even in challenging moments. I want you to take this Bible, read through it, and consider the teachings of forgiveness and humility that it holds. Think about what Jesus would do in this situation. It's not just about apologizing for something you didn't do, but it's about showing grace and compassion to others, even when it's tough." He held out the Bible toward Wayne. "And I'm also giving you this." He took hold of Wayne's other hand and pressed a crumpled twenty-dollar bill in it. "Consider it severance pay. I wish I could give you more, but right now it's not possible."

Wayne's hands fisted on both the Bible and the money. Frustration still overwhelmed him. He understood Mr. Bradley's intentions, but the weight of his emotions seemed too heavy to overcome. He looked down at the Bible and the crumpled bill in his hands, the conflict within him evident in his clenched fists and the way that he couldn't seem to unclench them. "You've given me a lot to think about," he murmured, his voice tinged with a mix of resignation and lingering resentment. He still just didn't understand why grace was reserved for a man like Mr. Miller but not for him. Why was it that he always seemed to receive the short end of the stick in life?

With a hard heart Wayne shoved them both into his back pockets and took hold of his gelding's reins. After placing a foot in the rawhide stirrup, he pushed off the ground and swung into the saddle. Tears stung his eyes as he turned his horse back toward town. What was he going to do now? Getting a job wasn't easy for an ex-con like himself, and he was only able to get this job through his connection with Mason Bradley. His hips and back moved with the motion of his horse's steps, even though Wayne's eyes were downcast toward the ground. What he needed was a fresh start. He needed to go someplace where no one knew his name and no one could find out about his past. As he was riding, it occurred to him that he might be crazy, but what if he joined that wagon train that was leaving on Monday morning? What if he talked to the wagon master and asked to help work the cattle until they made it to Oregon. Perhaps he could earn enough to buy land for cheap, the way everyone says it was available there. He sat up a little straighter and perked up at the thought.

What did he have to lose? Nothing.

Maybe that was enough to make such a crazy decision. He made his way directly to the office of the wagon master, but found it closed, since it was only Sunday evening. Pushing back his hat from his forehead, Wayne wiped the sweat off that he found there with the end of his sleeve. He frowned at the dirt there. If things hadn't gone all wonky, he'd have done his laundry today after church. Now he was wearing clothing that was filthy, and probably smelly, and if he was able to join the wagon train in the morning, he wasn't sure when he'd next be able to get his things washed.

He shook his head. Was he really already making plans to join the train? He wasn't even sure yet that the wagon master would accept him. What if the train was full? What if Wayne had already gotten a reputation because of what had happened with him and Mr. Miller, or even rumors about how he'd been in prison. He let out a breath and slumped in the saddle. This was a dumb idea, but what choice did he have? And what if the wagon master just plain told him "no?" What would he do? Not to mention he wasn't sure if he'd have enough money to buy land once he got to Oregon. He'd need at least a hundred dollars...maybe two. Wayne was at a loss. He really had no idea. His eggs were all in one basket here, and he had no choice but to let everything fall into place or let everything fall apart.

"Mr. Cody!" a voice shouted from behind him.

Frowning, Wayne turned around to find Mr. Browne approaching him with a wide grin. Wayne tipped his hat and dismounted his horse. There was nothing more rude than remaining mounted while an unmounted man was having a conversation with him. Wayne'd been on the receiving end of one of those snubs and he didn't much like it. Right now, though he was feeling hopeful, as just seeing Mr. Browne and knowing that he'd done right by the man lifted his spirits. It didn't matter what the results were, if he'd been given the choice to do right and get fired or do wrong and stay at the ranch, he'd choose to help all over again. Gripping his reins in his gloved hand, he greeted the older gentleman. "Mr. Browne. How are you?"

The older man removed his hat and wiped his brow as he finally reached him, his grin still wide as he nodded. "Good, good. I hope you're well, too, young man?"

Wayne cast a glance at the wagon master's office again but nodded. He really didn't want to get into the details of what he was feeling at the moment.

Mr. Browne nodded with him and then replaced his hat as he looked up and drew a more serious expression on his face. He pinned Wayne with his glare and stared at him for a long couple of seconds.

Shifting his weight from one foot to the other, Wayne began to feel a bit uncomfortable and wondered if he should say something.

Finally, Mr. Browne cleared his throat. "I need your help again, young man. Is there any chance that I could talk you into leaving Independence and joining my family on the wagon train in the morning?"

Blinking, Wayne felt pins and needles prickle along his shoulders. The weight that had been hanging over him there suddenly lifted. He almost laughed. "Yes, sir. I'd be more than grateful to join you. I was thinking about talking to the wagon master about joining the train as a cowboy, but was unsure if he was still hiring. If you need help with getting your family safe to Oregon, I'm more than happy to oblige."

The tension in Mr. Browne's shoulders seemed to loosen as his shoulders dropped a couple of inches, the man's broad smile came back. "That's wonderful. Yes, my family needs you." Then Mr. Browne's smile became a bit self-deprecating. "But there's one more small detail, a favor I must ask of you, Mr. Cody."

Frowning, Wayne asked, "What is it, sir?"

"Would you be willing to marry my daughter?"

To say that Wayne was shocked by this question would be an understatement. He froze where he stood, unable to speak, hardly able to stand, but definitely not able to move a single muscle. After a second or two, the spell broke. He blinked. "Excuse me, sir?"

Mr. Browne's eyes turned pleading. "For my son's health reasons, my family needs two wagons pulled on the train. I will drive one, and my daughter, Lily, is capable of driving the other. However, the wagon master will not let an unwed woman drive on his train, so we need you to help us. If you'd be willing to marry my daughter, and help us make it to Oregon, I'd be willing to pay you two hundred dollars. That would be more than enough for you to secure land once we get there. And it would be easy enough to find a judge to annul the marriage. You need not worry about performing any duties in the marriage. I just need you to help my family stay safe on the trail, that's all that I ask. Would you please do that for me? I'm desperate."

The whole time that the gentleman spoke, Wayne couldn't stop blinking. His brain was having trouble interpreting what the man was saying. Mr. Browne wanted him to marry his daughter, to help her on the trail and then get unmarried once they made it to Oregon. Even though his throat felt dry, Wayne managed to ask quietly, "So the situation is temporary... like a job?"

"Yes. Absolutely. I just need you to help keep my daughter and son safe for the journey. I don't expect anything more of you," Mr. Browne said, still wringing his hat in his hands, his eyes like those of someone desperately begging.

Wayne was still unsure. "But will your daughter be amenable to it? I'm not... I'm not a handsome man."

Mr. Browne nodded. "She understands the need for the arrangement."

Who was Wayne kidding? He wanted a fresh start, but here he was, unable to live with himself thinking that he could hide things from just the Browne family. After taking a deep breath, Wayne decided that if he was going to go through with this, he needed to disclose everything. "There's something you don't know about me, Mr. Browne. I'm not a good man, like you think I am. I've just been released from prison after serving ten years for manslaughter."

Mr. Browne's eyes widened. "Did you do it?"

Wayne shook his head. "It was an accident, but no, I wasn't even the one who pulled the trigger."

Nodding, Mr. Browne's eyes closed for a minute and then opened again with acceptance. "I believe you, son. I could tell you were a good man from the moment I saw you in the saloon. You weren't drinking or carousing, just eating a simple meal. Then you helped me when the livery man wanted to price gouge me. You stepped in, when you didn't have to. I saw you at church this morning, too. I wanted to talk to you about this then, but it seemed another gentleman had some words to discuss with you, so I held my tongue. I believe that it was providence that I ran into you just now. I was beginning to think that my family wasn't going to be able to leave on the wagon train in the morning. I was just taking a walk, praying and asking the Lord for some guidance, and here you were."

Providence. Guidance. Was that what the Lord was giving Wayne right now, too? Maybe it was His hand that had kept Wayne from pulling the trigger when he'd felt he'd had nowhere to go. Maybe this whole thing had been planned by God from the beginning just to lead him to this moment, and to help Wayne move all the way to Oregon. Even though Mr. Browne now knew of Wayne's past, the man was willing to look past it and hire him in this capacity to look after his family. Maybe more people in Oregon would be willing to allow Wayne that fresh start, too. For the first time in a while, he was feeling truly hopeful. Finally, he nodded. "All right, Mr. Browne. If your daughter will have me, I'm willing to marry her."

CHAPTER 5

"Get up, Lily," her father whispered, "There's something we need to do."

Lily was pulled from her sleep, and for half a moment, she could barely open her eyes. But when she saw that it was still pitch black out, she sat with a start and a gasp, immediately looking to her right to see if her brother was okay. Thomas lay sleeping next to her still, his face peaceful looking in the light of the moon from the window. She blinked hard and turned to her father who had shaken her shoulder and whispered, "What's going on? What time is it?"

"Hurry and get dressed. I'll be waiting for you outside," was all he said before slipping out of the room.

Confused and groggy, but her heart still racing,

Lily pulled the coverlet from her legs and set her feet upon the cold, hardwood floor. She picked up the clock from the mantle and took it to the window so that she could use the light from outside to read the time. Eleven forty-five. She'd only been asleep for about three hours. What on earth could her father want her to do so late in the night? Her brain remained in a fog as she went behind the dressing screen and got dressed as quickly as she could in the light she had from outside, afraid to light a lantern and wake Thomas for no reason. After she'd buttoned the top of her shoes, she started for the hallway. The moonlight cast eerie shadows in the room, and a sense of urgency hung in the air. The clock ticked closer to midnight, leaving Lily wondering about the mysterious task her father had called her for as she grabbed her shawl and pulled open the door.

Her father stood in the hallway, offering her a smile as soon as he saw her. "Your hair," was all that he said as he gestured toward the gilded mirror that sat in the hallway.

Lily glanced at her reflection in the mirror, her confusion deepening. Her hair was a mess from sleep, and she quickly ran her fingers through it, trying to tame the unruly strands. "Why is my hair so important right now?" she wondered aloud, her voice a whisper.

Father's smile turned enigmatic, and he reached into his pocket, producing a small blue ribbon. "Here's a piece of your mother's ribbon I keep with me. You can borrow it...something blue," he said softly, stepping closer and gently tying the ribbon around Lily's wrist. "I'm not one for all the traditions, but maybe this will bring us a little bit of luck."

Lily studied the ribbon, its color pale in the glow of the lantern in the hallway. Questions swirled in her mind, but her father's serious expression made her hold them back. Once he finished, he looked her up and down with a sigh and then took her by the hand. She frowned at him as they started away. "What's going on, Father?"

"Come on, they are waiting for us."

"Who?" she asked as she followed him to the stairway.

"You'll see," he answered as he released her hand and then guided her shoulder toward the stairs.

Frowning harder, she continued to go where he led her through the quiet foyer of the hotel, where not a soul milled about. No wonder since it had to be a little after midnight now. When he opened the front door and gestured for her to go through first, her confusion grew, but she stepped through and into the light chill of the evening air, glad that she'd opted to bring her shawl. Her father turned to the right and started across the quiet street. It was the first time she'd seen the street without a single horse, wagon, or carriage to wait for before crossing. He stepped down into the dirt, but her feet remained still. When he turned back toward her, she asked, "What is going on, Father? It's the middle of the night. What could we possibly need to do right now before we leave tomorrow?"

He let out a sigh and then looked down at his hands. "Remember when I said I would take care of that situation I told you about. In order for us to take two wagons on the train, the wagon master said that you had to be wed, correct?"

She furrowed her brows. "Yes..." Her heart raced, and she looked at her father with a mix of surprise and disbelief. "Wait, are you saying... you want me to get married? Tonight?"

Her father nodded solemnly, his gaze meeting hers. "I know it's sudden, Lily, but it's the only way we can secure passage for both wagons on the train tomorrow. It's an arrangement of convenience, a necessary formality. I've arranged everything, and the groom is waiting for us."

Lily's mind raced as she tried to understand what she was being told. She didn't know what to say, the shock knocking the wind out of her. Her father put a hand on her shoulder and started guiding her once more. Then she realized the direction they were heading. "Are we going to the church?"

Her father nodded again, his expression a mix of reassurance and urgency. "Yes, the groom is waiting for us there, and I believe this arrangement will benefit us all."

Lily's heart pounded in her chest. She felt a rush of emotions, ranging from disbelief to anxiety to a hint of curiosity. This was certainly not what she had expected when her father woke her in the middle of the night. And when he said that he would take care of it, she was certain he meant that he would convince the wagon master or make other arrangements. Ones that didn't include her becoming a bride. She stopped walking forward, took a deep breath, trying to steady herself. "And what if I refuse?"

Her father's gaze softened, and he reached out to gently touch her arm. "Lily, I wouldn't ask this of you if I didn't believe it was necessary. I know it's a lot to take in, but we're facing challenges, and this is a way to ensure our future. I have found a trustworthy young man who is willing to help and protect our family on the trail. And it doesn't need to be permanent. You and Mr. Cody will get an annulment once we reach Oregon. "

"Mr. Cody..." she whispered as she looked between her father and the church standing in the distance. She thought about the journey they were about to take, the uncertain times that lay ahead, and the responsibilities that rested on her shoulders. Thomas needed to move to the west coast for his health. There were children out west who needed a teacher. Her father needed a fresh start. And with all of these, they needed to take the two wagons to help with the travels. If this gentleman—Mr. Cody would help and protect her family, then it would be worth it. And besides, if he's a good man who sticks to his word, and her father trusted him, then she should, too. With a determined nod, she turned back to her father. "Alright, Father. If this is what we need to do, then I'll do it. For our family."

Tears glistened in her father's eyes as he pulled her into a hug. "Everything will be all right, Lily. You'll see."

With her heart racing, Lily found herself already looking up the steps of the church. The window showed that there were lanterns lit within. Her father started up the steps and she followed him with heavy footsteps, unsure if she was doing the right thing. She was going to swear before God and the church that she would not part from this man until death—while knowing in her heart that it was a temporary, convenient situation.

As her father pushed open the heavy wooden door to the church and looked back at her, she steeled herself. Maybe this situation was a lie, but it was also a solution to the problem they were facing. Perhaps it was providence that led her and this "Mr. Cody" to come together. She blinked and stopped before entering the church and looked up at her father. "What's his first name? How can I marry someone without even knowing that much about him."

Her father looked down upon her with sad eyes that looked as though they might well up with tears at any moment. "It's Wayne," he said, his voice cracking a bit.

"Wayne Cody," she said, took a deep breath, and started into the church building.

THE FRONT DOORS OF THE CHURCH CREAKED OPEN, and Wayne's gaze shot toward the front of the building. His hands were clenched into fists, and sweat had wet his palms. Nervous barely described how he felt. He was mortified. Why had he ever agreed to this? Mr. Browne appeared in the doorway of the church, looking back toward the steps, speaking to someone, presumably Wayne's bride.

He swallowed hard at the thought. His bride? How could he even think such a thing? This lady was just as likely to walk in, take one look at Wayne's scarred face and run from the building. With his crooked nose and scarred cheek, he knew he was ugly. He looked like a bulldog who'd been in a few too many fights. Truth be told, he was exactly that. Someone could easily mistake him for a drunkard and a pugilist, even though he was neither one. His heart raced in his chest and darkness crowded his vision. Did he feel faint? He feared that he just might.

The anticipation in the church was palpable, and Wayne's anxiety continued to mount as the moments passed. His mind raced with doubt and insecurity, and he couldn't shake the feeling that this entire situation was a mistake. He clenched and unclenched his fists, the sweat on his palms making them clammy. He shifted uncomfortably, his eyes fixed on the entrance as he awaited the arrival of his unexpected bride.

A shuffle came from the front of the church, and Wayne's breath caught in his throat as he saw her enter. His heart stopped. It was the girl from the general store, the same one who had looked him full in the face and still offered a smile. How could it be her of all people? His heart sank. Would she look at him differently now, knowing that they were about to become more than strangers. Each step she took toward him, the more nervous he became. She walked with a mixture of determination and uncertainty, and when her eyes met his briefly, there was no disdain there as he feared there might be, and then she glanced away. Wayne's heart pounded in his chest, and he wiped his palms on his dungarees.

As she drew nearer, Wayne caught sight of her delicate features and the wariness in her eyes. His heart ached for her, knowing that she had been pulled into this situation just as unexpectedly as he had. And now she was going to be stuck with him. Why couldn't it have been a plain woman? Someone other than her. Her blonde hair shone in the lantern light and sparkled like gold. Her blue eyes were stormier than the sunset sky after the rain. She was the most beautiful woman that he'd ever seen, and he knew that he was likely the ugliest man that she'd ever seen, and yet she showed no recoil.

Mr. Browne led her toward Wayne, a sympathetic smile on his face. "Lily, meet Wayne," he said gently, his voice carrying a hint of reassurance.

Wayne managed a small, nervous smile, trying to appear as friendly as he could despite the turmoil within and what his twisted face might look like to her. "Hello…" he croaked and then cleared his throat and tried again. "Hello, Lily."

Lily's eyes met his again, and Wayne saw a mixture of emotions flicker across her face. But none of them were the repugnance that he expected. He wondered what she might be thinking, feared that she would look upon him with abhorrence at any moment. Instead, her soft eyes looked over his features and seemed determined to go through with this marriage of convenience. If she was determined, there had to be good reason. And after all, Wayne had promised Mr. Browne that he would help and protect their family on the trail and that is what he would be determined to do as well.

Steeling himself, he extended a slightly trembling hand towards her, offering a gesture of greeting. "I know this is all rather sudden and unusual," he began, his voice surprisingly steady. "But I promise, I'll do my best to make this arrangement as tolerable as possible."

Lily hesitated for a moment before tentatively placing her hand in his. Her touch was gentle, and Wayne felt a jolt of connection that surprised him. He offered her a small, genuine smile, hoping to ease some of the tension that hung in the air.

"Thank you, Wayne," she whispered, her voice carrying a hint of vulnerability and ringing through his body like a bell. Everything about her seemed fragile in that moment, and Wayne's urge to protect her intensified.

The minister stepped forward, his kind eyes resting on both of them. "Shall we begin?"

Wayne nodded, his grip on Lily's hand tightening only slightly as they turned their attention to the minister. As the ceremony began, Wayne's mind focused on the solemn words being exchanged, and resolve filled his heart. Whatever challenges lay ahead, he was committed to facing them for Lily and her family.

"Do you have the rings?" the minister asked.

Mr. Browne cleared his throat and then produced two gold bands. When Lily saw them, her breath caught, and tears welled in her eyes. She shook her head. "No. Those... those are yours and... and Mother's"

Tears filled Mr. Browne's eyes too, but he had a soft smile and said, "It's okay, Lily. I couldn't procure rings on such a short notice, and this would make your mother happy as well."

Pulling her hand out of Wayne's light grip, she swiped at her eyes and then fisted her hands at her sides. "You can't. This is wrong... it's all wrong."

Wayne's heart sank. She was right. This was wrong. He wanted the job to protect their family for the money so that he could purchase land when they made it to Oregon at first. But when he saw who Mr. Browne's daughter was, he became steadfast in his conviction that he would protect her and their family, but this whole marriage being a sham... if she couldn't do it, than neither could he.

Mr. Browne took hold of Lily's fist. "I promise you, this is for the best. Wayne Cody is a good man."

Lily glanced up at Wayne once before returning her determined gaze to her father. "But you hardly know him. How can you be so sure?"

"I prayed about it. I prayed about this for days, Lily. This wasn't some small decision. I knew that. I was willing to forego the wagon train—intended to. Planning for you and me to take our two wagons and brave the trail without them." His gaze shot toward the minister and he nodded. "I was here in the church several times, asking God to protect us while we went it alone. But then God sent Wayne. And he is a good man. I know it in my heart and believe it utterly. You can trust me in that. I arranged this marriage only after I knew that it was providence and not before. Your mother would approve. I know that too."

Lily shook her head as tears started down her cheeks.

Wayne wanted to end this. He hated seeing this beautiful lady cry.

Slowly and gently, Mr. Browne pried open his daughters fingers and placed the two gold rings into her hand. "But still, I leave it up to you."

For a long moment, Lily stared at the two wedding bands in her hand, and Wayne almost held his breath, wondering what she might do with them. Then she closed her fingers around them, fisting her hand again. With a deep breath, she turned toward Wayne and met eyes with him with more resolve than she'd had a moment before. She held out her hand. "Here are the rings."

The minister nodded toward Wayne, and in response, Wayne took the smaller of the two rings and then repeated the vows after the minister. Once the vows were spoken, he placed the ring upon her finger. Then Lily did the same, speaking her vows with a strong, determined voice and then placed the ring gently upon his finger as well. Wayne was amazed that both the rings fit as though they were made for the two of them.

"Now you may kiss the bride."

Wayne's heart stopped again. He'd forgotten about that part.

As the weight of the moment settled in, his heart began to pound in his chest. He stepped closer to Lily, and he could feel the intensity of her gaze on him, her eyes searching his face. With a mixture of trepidation and longing, he lifted his hand and gently cupped her cheek, his thumb brushing against her soft skin. His scarred face felt hot under her observation, and he could see uncertainty in her eyes. But that uncertainty wasn't because of his scars or his crooked nose. She seemed uncertain if she could go through with this command of a kiss. Even he could feel that. He wanted to reassure her, so he leaned in slowly, giving her the chance to pull away if she wished. And then he turned her cheek just slightly to place his lips gently right next to her lips. Still, something shifted in the air around them.

The world seemed to fade away, leaving only the two of them standing in that moment. Wayne's heart raced, but a sense of warmth spread through his chest. He felt Lily's fingers curl around the fabric of his shirt, her touch both gentle and urgent. The kiss was soft and chaste, but it seemed a spark ignited between them.

For a brief moment, Wayne forgot about the circumstances that had brought them together. He forgot about his scars, his doubts, and his fears. All that mattered was the sensation of her skin against his lips, her body heat against his, the touch of her hands, and the unspoken promise that they were in this together. The kiss felt like a promise of solidarity, a vow to face whatever challenges lay ahead.

As the kiss came to an end, they pulled away slightly, their breaths mingling in the cool night air. Wayne looked into Lily's eyes, his heart still racing, but now with a different kind of anticipation. He saw a mixture of emotions in her gaze—surprise, curiosity, and perhaps a hint of something more. He offered her a small, genuine smile, hoping that the connection they had just shared would provide some comfort in this unexpected situation.

The minister's voice broke the moment, reminding them of their surroundings. Wayne reluctantly stepped back, his hand falling away from Lily's cheek. He glanced at Mr. Browne, who was watching them with a mixture of approval and understanding. It seemed that the emotional journey they had just embarked on had not gone unnoticed.

With a nod from the minister, the ceremony continued, sealing their commitment to each other. Despite the unconventional circumstances, Wayne felt he was willing to face whatever challenges came their way, to protect and support Lily and her family as they journeyed westward.

CHAPTER 6

May 1, 1854

INDEPENDENCE

A fog misted the air, too thick for the rising sun to pass through without scattering golden rays of light in all directions. Wayne had barely slept, even though it was on a featherbed in a hotel room across the hall from his bride. It was the softest, most comfortable bed he'd been in for as long as he could remember, and yet sleep had eluded him almost entirely. As a result, he was up and getting things ready before the sun and most of the town. Still, it wasn't long until Mr. Browne joined him.

Together, the two of them hitched the oxen to

one of the wagons and the mules to the other. All the family's belongings were loaded into the oxen's cart, and the other cart had been left empty with the exception of the water barrel that was loaded onto every cart, a shotgun and shells, and bedding material to make the ride as comfortable as possible for Mr. Browne's son, who Wayne had yet to meet.

Once they'd finished, the fog had lifted a little, but enough remained that he couldn't see for more than about fifty yards. Mr. Cooper, the wagon master came over to them to give some final instructions and advice for the journey ahead. "Morning, Mr. Browne," he greeted him with a nod, his voice carrying a tone of experience. "Looks like we've got some fog to contend with today. Best keep your eyes sharp and your animals steady. Would either of you like a cup of coffee or a biscuit? We're taking a chuck wagon with us to maintain supplies and a herd of cattle. We just ask that everyone who hunts is also willing to share what they can with the rest of the camp as well. This is how we've successfully made four crossings on the trail with minimal losses."

Mr. Browne looked over at Wayne and nodded. The two of them followed Mr. Cooper over to the chuck wagon, its wooden frame adorned with pots, pans, and various supplies. The aroma of freshly brewed coffee and warm biscuits wafted through the air, providing a comforting contrast to the lingering fog. Wayne and Mr. Browne gratefully accepted the offered cups of coffee and biscuits, savoring the simple pleasure before the journey ahead. Once finished they offered the empty cups back to the cook who took them and threw them into a wash basin. When Wayne turned back toward their wagons, Lily and her brother stepped through the fog.

Wayne's heart skipped a beat at the sight of her, and for a moment, all he could do was stare at her. She looked ethereal, the golden rays of sun dispersing through the fog and giving her a halo... a glow about her whole body. When she caught sight of Wayne and her father, a smile spread across her lips and she guided her younger brother toward them. The younger boy pulled his father and sister closer to him and embraced them both together. "Family hug!" He declared as the family squeezed each other tightly.

A touch of longing pricked at Wayne's heart. He'd never had the opportunity to pull in his mother and father in such a way. The concept of family togetherness was foreign to him.

"Morning," Lily greeted him once released, her

quiet voice carrying a melodic tone that seemed to match the tranquility of the scene.

Her father beamed at them, laying a hand upon his son's shoulder. "Did you eat breakfast yet?"

The boy nodded, but barely cast a glance toward his father, as his serious face studied Wayne.

"Morning, Lily," Wayne replied, feeling a bit shy. He wasn't sure how to greet his new bride. Bride. That was a word he'd never thought he'd use to describe any woman, especially not a lady as elegant or as beautiful as Lily.

She nodded to him and offered a shy smile. "This is my younger brother, Thomas," Lily said, placing a reassuring hand on Thomas's shoulder. "Thomas, this is Wayne Cody."

Wayne extended his hand to Thomas. "Nice to meet you, Thomas."

Thomas eyed his hand, but then offered a shy smile and a nod in response. "Nice to meet you too, Mr. Cody."

Wayne shook his head. "If you don't mind, I'd prefer if you call me Wayne."

The boy's brow furrowed, and he looked up at his sister as if to ask permission. She nodded and so Thomas's gaze returned to Wayne as he nodded again and answered, "All right. Wayne."

A whistle blew toward the front of the wagons and a shout filled the air. "Mount up!"

The sudden sharp sounds and shouts made Wayne's apprehension intensify. He nervously adjusted his hat, casting a quick glance at Lily before focusing on the task at hand. Mr. Browne, however, took charge with a reassuring smile.

"Alright, Wayne," Mr. Browne said in a hearty voice. "Let's make sure everything's secured and ready to go."

Wayne nodded, his throat feeling a bit tight. He busied himself with the final preparations, occasionally stealing glances at Lily and her younger brother, Thomas. The boy seemed preoccupied, his expression distant as he stared at the ground and kicked at a rock that sat in the dirt.

Lily's presence beside Wayne was both comforting and intimidating, and he struggled to find something to say to her, knowing that he wanted to break this barrier between the two of them in some way. Finally, he managed to ask, "Are you ready to go?"

Her brows scrunched a bit as she peered up at him, then she shrugged. "Ready as I could ever be, I suppose."

He swallowed, unsure how to respond.

Then Mr. Browne clapped him on the back. "Let's get started. The sooner we get on the trail, the sooner we reach Oregon, right?"

A nervous laugh bubbled up from Wayne's gut, and heat filled his cheeks at the sound of it. His gaze darted toward Lily, but she just smiled and nodded toward him as though giving permission for Wayne to be himself. He smiled wider in the moment, allowing Mr. Browne's jovial spirit to infect him as well. Then he asked Lily, "Do you need a hand getting into the wagon?"

She shook her head. "No, I'll be fine."

And then she guided her brother's shoulder toward the wagon pulled by the mules. Thomas's gaze flickered toward Wayne for a moment before he looked away, his brows furrowing slightly. It seemed the boy wasn't sure what to make of Wayne and this whole situation that was likely not explained to him fully, since he was only a child. Wayne couldn't blame him for feeling strange over the situation.

Once Lily and Thomas were in their cart, and Mr. Browne led the oxen, Wayne untied his gelding's reins from the back of the cart and mounted up in one quick motion. Thomas's eyes went wide from the seat of the cart. He blinked. "You look like a real cowboy."

Wayne tipped his head toward the boy. "I am one," he said and offered a wink.

The boy quickly turned away, but the tips of his ears gave away the pink tinge that likely covered his whole face. Lily laughed and took up her reins with a deft hand, guiding her mules in the direction that her father's oxen had started in.

Once the wagons started to roll, the atmosphere buzzed with anticipation. And the journey began, the rhythmic creaking of wheels and the soft jingle of buckles on harnesses filling the air. As they moved forward, Wayne's thoughts were a mix of apprehension and a determination to prove himself to both Lily and her family. He knew that earning the trust and respect of Mr. Browne and his new bride wouldn't be easy, but he was ready to face the challenges ahead, one step at a time.

LILY PULLED THE MULES' REINS, HEARING THE collective "whoa" from several wagons ahead. She gave the mules a deep whoa in response so that the wagons behind her could also hear. Her wagon drew to a halt with a few feet to spare between her and her father's wagon just ahead.

"Whoa," a deep voice said from the horse that had been riding alongside her wagon. "Whoa!" he shouted louder and reined his horse toward the back of the wagon, taking off like a shot.

Confused, Lily stood up in the wagon and looked behind them. She watched as Wayne grabbed hold of the ox that had been at the lead of the wagon behind her just before it had gored the back of her wagon. Her heart skipped in her chest. If the ox had been allowed to continue it would have damaged their wagon and perhaps some of the contents within. Her brother had gone to lay down a couple hours before then, and their water barrel was at the back of the wagon as well. Trying to still her heart, her hand fluttered to her chest. Thank the Lord that Wayne had been able to stop the ox behind them in time.

The gentleman behind them apologized to both Wayne and to her with a forlorn look upon his face. "I wasn't paying attention," he said. "I won't let it happen again."

"It's all right," she called back toward them. "No harm done."

But there could have been. Had she not called out the "Whoa" loud enough for the man behind her to hear? Was it her fault? She'd need to make sure that she said it louder, and perhaps more than once next time to be certain.

Wayne rode back over toward her, his eyes intense. He'd been just as affected by the near accident as she had been. Throughout the long day, Wayne had hardly said two words to her. He just rode alongside them quietly, running ahead on occasion, lagging behind on others. He'd gotten them lunch at the chuck wagon and brought it back to both Lily and Thomas, saying little more than a "welcome" at their thanks.

"Thank you," she said with relief when he reached her.

He nodded and tipped his hat. "If you'd like to go get supper with your father, I'll take care of the mules and his oxen too."

She frowned. "We can't ask you to do all of that."

"Well, ma'am, you didn't ask, but I'm offering."

She tilted her head and lifted a brow. "Do you often hear grooms calling their wives ma'am? Besides, am I even old enough to be called a ma'am?"

This time, it was Wayne's turn to frown. "You're right. I should call you by name."

She nodded.

"But, it also wasn't quite right to call you miss,

73

either. Since even though you're young, you're not exactly Miss Browne anymore." Even as he said it, his face turned bright red. To hide his discomfiture, he cast his gaze away from her as he dismounted and started toward the mules.

Heat rose to her face as she realized that he was right. She wasn't a "miss" anymore. In fact—for now —she wasn't even a Browne. Mrs. Cody? Her heart thumped in her chest at the thought and the heat in her cheeks intensified. That was her name now. In fact anyone in the wagon train might be inclined to call her just that. And she'd have to answer to it. She let out a breath and patted her cheeks, trying to get herself to calm down.

A jostle from the back of the wagon got her attention away from her own lack of composure. Thomas popped up, looking a little tired, but not quite as exhausted as he had earlier. "Is it supper time?" he asked around a yawn.

"It is," she said as she helped him out of the back of the wagon and onto the seat. "Are you hungry?"

"There's something about this journey," Thomas said. "I feel like I haven't done anything all day except sit around and lay down and sleep, but I'm starving."

She huffed a laugh and leaned in toward him, whispering as though it were a secret, "Me too."

The sun hung low on the horizon but hadn't quite set yet. They likely had an hour until dark, which would lend them all enough light to get supper and make camp. Wayne had unharnessed the two mules from the wagon and was leading them off toward the grazing area with hobbles in his hand. He really had done everything without a bit of help from her. Father came around the wagon at about that time and spoke to Wayne in tones that she couldn't quite make out. Then he made his way toward her. "That was an eventful day, wasn't it? I'd swear we must have made it more than twenty miles, but the wagon master says that we'll average somewhere around twelve to fifteen a day."

He reached up and offered a hand to help her down from the cart. Placing her hand in his, she scooted closer to the edge and then gripped his hand as she stepped down. He held her waist with the other hand. Once she was down, her father released her and then helped swing down Thomas as well. Lily couldn't help but cast a glance over in the direction of where her "fake" husband had taken the mules.

"He's taking them to get a drink of water at the

river and then he'll let them graze. Once he's done taking care of them, he'll get the oxen, too." Her father must have seen her worried glance.

"Is that really fair, father? It's supposed to be our job to take care of the animals before we eat dinner, isn't it."

"He offered to do it." Father shrugged. "I certainly don't expect him to do this every day, but it was kind of him to offer for this once."

Lily frowned. "Too kind. Could you take Thomas to the chuck wagon, Father? I'm going to tend to the oxen."

He blinked. "What?"

She lifted up her skirts and tied them up in such a way that they reached only half way down her calves instead of down to her ankles. Then she pulled her hair up a little tighter and tied her bonnet string around it. "You heard me, Father," she replied and started toward the oxen. Then she called over her shoulder. "Take care of Thomas."

When she reached the oxen, she looked over the buckles on the harness and found it similar to a horse's girth. Although she didn't have much experience with oxen, she did with horses, and felt that they couldn't be horribly different, could they? Once she freed one of them, she led it away from the other two. They mewed at the ox that was leaving sounding woeful that he was going off without them. Then the ox that she was leading stopped dead in its tracks and refused to move. Frustrated, Lily tugged a bit harder on the lead. The ox grunted, stretched his neck out, but refused to set one foot forward.

"I told your father that I would handle that," a deep, kind voice said from right behind her, causing a shiver to course through her body and goose flesh to rise on her arms. Slowly, she turned to face him, feeling her cheeks flush in embarrassment that he had caught her trying to handle the oxen on her own and failing miserably at it.

"Oh, I...I know you said you'd take care of them," Lily stammered, keeping her eyes downcast as she continued holding the ox's lead. "I just thought, well, that I should help too..." Her voice trailed off uncertainly.

An awkward silence fell between them. Both were very aware that they barely knew each other, despite already being husband and wife. She snuck a peek up at him, the thought of their chaste kiss in the church coming back to her when her gaze reached his lips. Her fists clenched around the ox's lead rope. Why on earth would she think about such a thing at a time like this? Butterflies fluttered in her stomach as her nervousness rose.

Wayne rubbed the back of his neck, also seeming just as unsure as she was about how to act. "It's alright ma'am—I mean, Lily," he corrected. "I don't mind doing the work."

"But you're not just an errand boy." She swallowed hard, her next words coming out hoarse. "This is all of our responsibility... and we are married, so we should be partners, shouldn't we?" Lily asked hesitantly, sneaking a glance up at him.

"Yes, of course," Wayne said quickly, blinking at her with wide eyes. "This is all still new and I'm not quite certain what's right and what's not in this situation."

She nodded. "Neither am I. I guess we'll learn as we go along." Then she tugged on the ox's lead. "But right now, I need to get this ox moving so that he can get a drink of water and rest, but he's not cooperating."

"Now that, I can handle," he said with a genuine, confident smile. "You see, oxen are herd animals, so they don't like going anywhere alone. If they are alone, then a predator can get them, but together, they feel safe. Hold him here a minute."

Wayne unhitched the two remaining oxen and

led them over toward her. They mooed to each other in what seemed like relief. Suddenly, Lily felt a bit guilty for trying to take away one of the three and worrying the others.

"There. Now that they are all together, let's see if we can go get them some water," he said as he offered her another smile and started pulling the two oxen that he had toward the river.

This time, when Lily pulled the lead rope, the ox who'd been so stubborn the moment before came along readily. She shook her head at the black beast and then followed Wayne to the river. They had to traverse through ankle deep mud before reaching the water. The animals all drank from the river which moved at a slow pace and swirled around their muzzles. Lilly peered across to the other side, where it just seemed like open grasslands. The sun had lowered a bit more, casting a golden hue over everything. "It's so peaceful out here, I could almost forget that there's a wagon train nearby except for that low rumble. This isn't much like the city."

Wayne smiled up at her while rolling up his sleeve which had fallen. "No, it's not."

"How do you know so much about oxen?"

A shrug, a cast glance toward the ox and then toward the other side of the river. "I was raised on a farm. I don't know much about anything except horses and cattle. I guess that's why I thought it would be more useful for me to go ahead and take care of the animals." He gestured toward her feet. "And I guess I didn't expect you'd be wanting to get your shoes all muddy like that."

She looked down at her own feet, seeing that the mud was indeed deep. Shaking her head, she waved it off with a hand and a giggle. "Don't you know? All the girls trudge in mud like this. It's one of our favorite pastimes."

His brow furrowed in confusion, then he chuckled. "I'm sure."

Lifting a foot, and feeling the mud nearly suck off her shoe, she wondered exactly how she was going to get that boot clean afterward. Then she set the foot back down. It wasn't something she needed to think about now. For now, she'd just enjoy the peacefulness of their surroundings, the easy happiness of the animals getting their food and drink, and the fact that she was helping instead of just sitting around and letting Wayne do all of the work.

AFTER THE OXEN HAD GOTTEN THEIR FILL OF THE river, Wayne started to lead his toward the designated grazing area. In truth, he was happy to have had Lily stay behind and help him. He wasn't sure if the oxen would have been so easy to lead if he'd had three of them in his hand at once, which he would have had to do in order to keep the herd of them together. Her presence was both comforting and discomforting at the same time. When he was keeping himself busy, he liked having her nearby, but when he'd sit still and think about how close she was, his anxiety rose. She was so pretty, and he still marveled at how he didn't repel her on sight as he seemed to do even with the other women on the wagon train. He saw how they recoiled when he came around them on his horse. They seemed to look on him with fear as though he were some kind of outlaw or bandit. But Lily was different than them. She smiled at him. When was the last time a woman besides his mother smiled at him? Perhaps back when he was fifteen, before that turkey hunt went the wrong way, and he ended up in jail. There were girls who used to look at him admiringly back then. But with his scarred and beat up face, all that had changed.

"Whoa," Lily said, her arm swinging as she

reeled, trying to get her footing as they made their way out of the mud.

Quickly, Wayne reached out and took hold of her arm to help steady her. Her grip took hold and tightened on his forearm as she worked to get her footing again. Once she had a foot on dry ground, she peered up at him with a self-deprecating smile.

"Sorry about that."

He nodded, the lump in his throat stealing anything he might say. When she tried to release her hold, he frowned. "It's all right. Keep hold until you're out of the muddy bank."

"All right," she said, taking hold of his arm again as she navigated the last two steps out of the mud. Then she released him. "Thank you so much."

Again, he nodded, unsure his words wouldn't betray him somehow. Together the two of them led the oxen over to where the mules were grazing along with some of the other animals that had made it to the designated area already. Lily held the animals while Wayne applied the walking hobbles to each of the animals' legs so that they wouldn't wander overnight. Then he straightened himself and helped remove the halters from their heads. He took hold of all the lead ropes as well and swung them over his shoulder. As he passed by his bay gelding already grazing, he patted the horse on the rump.

"What's his name?" she asked, setting a hand on the horse's rump, just as he had. The horse swished his tail and walked a few steps away gaining distance from the annoying humans who were interrupting his meal.

Frowning he thought for a moment. The livery man back in Jefferson City had said what the gelding's name was, but Wayne hadn't thought on it since then. It took him a moment to remember. "It's Bingo, I think."

She lifted a brow. "You think?"

"Might have been Rover. I remember it was a common dog's name."

Tilting her head at him, she asked, "You don't remember?"

He shook his head slowly, feeling the disappointment in her eyes. "I'm pretty sure it's Bingo."

"Okay, then," she said, determined, and dusting off her hands by clapping them together. "We'll call him Bingo, then."

"Is it that important to you?"

"Well, if I need to refer to him, it's better than just calling him 'horse' or something. It's actually a little strange that you didn't ever call him anything."

He shrugged and started walking back toward camp. "It's not like I need to call him by name to have a conversation with him. He doesn't say my name, you know. In fact, most of our communication is done without ever talking at all."

Keeping up with his pace, she looked up at him, the disappointment in her eyes was completely replaced by a sparkle. "That's good. Riding is about where your weight is and how you apply pressure through your legs and hands on the reins. A horse can even feel the turn of your head, the weight of your body changes that much."

"How do you know so much about horses for a city girl who doesn't know about cows?"

She shrugged. "I rode horses on my grandfather's farm, but he didn't have cattle or any other animal really... other than dogs and cats."

"So that's why you can handle the mules on the cart?"

"That's why." She nodded.

Around them, the crickets had begun chirping as the last rays of sunlight cast a golden glow on everything around them. The cacophony of conversations from the camp at the wagons competed with the crickets, and someone played a jaunty tune on a harmonica not too far away. As they drew closer, the scent of supper wafted toward them on the light evening breeze, making Wayne's mouth water. It had been a long day, and his feelings of uncertainty and his duty to protect Mr. Browne's family had worn him out almost as much as the cattle did on the ranch. He led Lily over to the chuck wagon, meeting her father and younger brother along the way. They were already eating hearty bowls of stew.

"Grab a bowl, you two. Plenty to go around," Mr. Browne said cheerfully between bites.

At the chuck wagon, they stood in a short line and awaited their turn. It wasn't long before the cook ladled two bowls full of the fragrant beef stew with a biscuit and handed them to the pair. It was simple fare, but it smelled delicious after a long day on the trail. They found a place to sit near Lily's family and dug in. The stew tasted as good as it smelled; the beef was salty and tender, the potatoes and carrots perfectly cooked. Wayne finished his portion quickly, mopping up the last bit of gravy with the biscuit. Lily and her father kept up a quiet, yet jovial conversation while they finished what they were eating, and Thomas played with a stick, drawing in the dirt, his empty bowl set to the side.

A man was handing out pamphlets and approached their group. "Here, this could save your life," he said offering one to both Wayne and Mr. Browne.

Wayne took the pamphlet and looked at it frowning. He knew his letters, but had left school, years before he even went to prison. Ch-O-Lee-Ray was in big letters at the top of the pamphlet. He wasn't sure what that meant, and the rest of the letters were smaller and closer together, and he wasn't sure if he could interpret any of it.

"What's it say?" Lily asked, peering over at him.

Swallowing hard, he offered Lily the paper and said, "Read it for yourself."

After taking the pamphlet, Lily squinted at it. "I don't have my spectacles, so I can't read it, but it's about Cholera, right? I can barely make out that much."

Cholera. So that was what the paper was about.

"Yes," Mr. Browne said, looking up from the pamphlet. "It seems that the suggestion is that we should only drink cold water from wells or springs, and that all other water sources should be used in tea or coffee."

"Where does the water in the barrels come from?" Thomas asked, looking up from what he'd been drawing.

"Likely they were drawn from the well at Independence. There are wells at the forts and outposts on the trails, but most refill from the rivers when they run out of water," Mr. Browne answered with a shrug.

"I guess it's a good thing we like tea," Thomas said as he went back to drawing again on the ground.

Lily huffed a laugh. "I guess so."

The family sat around the campfire for a spell, listening to others talk about the journey thus far. It had only been a day, but it felt like they had traveled a great distance from Independence already. Overhead, the dark sky was dotted with so many stars in all directions and it seemed that the only light for miles and miles was the fire at the center of camp.

Before long, Thomas stood and tugged at his sister's sleeve. "I'm tired."

Lily had just finished stifling a yawn. "I'm pretty tired myself."

"I guess we should all consider turning in," Mr. Browne said as he slowly drew to his feet. "Tomorrow will be just as eventful as today, I'm sure. Wayne, would you give me a hand with erecting a tent?"

"Of course, sir," Wayne answered and then followed Mr. Browne to retrieve the canvas tent from the back of their wagon. Within minutes the small canvas tent had been erected.

Mr. Browne gestured toward the tent. "There's room in the tent for the two of us if you'd like to join me."

Wayne shrugged, looking back up at the sky. "I'm a cowboy, sir. I'm quite used to sleeping under the stars with a saddle for a pillow. It'll be nice just to not have to get up at a certain time to keep watch over the cattle."

"Can't say I'm disappointed." Mr. Browne laughed. "I was hoping you'd decline, as a man needs a little room to spread out."

"I'll bed down under the wagon, so I can keep watch over Lily and Thomas."

Mr. Browne patted him on the shoulder. "Good man. I thank you for protecting my family just as you promised."

Wayne nodded. "Good night, sir."

"Good night, son."

The two men parted ways, and Wayne headed back to the wagon where the hushed whispers of Lily and Thomas occupied the innards of the wagon bed. The two of them would be sharing the covered wagon for the trip, as they'd planned before the journey. Wayne pulled his saddle off the back of the wagon and set it on the ground just under the cart. Then he unhooked the bedroll from the back of the saddle and lay it out. Once finished, he crawled under the cart and rested his head against the saddle. The smell of leather and horse sweat offered comfort to him, and having a "roof" over his head gave him a feeling of warmth and protection.

"Good night, Lily," Thomas's voice said from above him. "And good night, Mr. Cody."

Wayne's face flushed. Did the two of them watch him crawl under the cart? He cleared his throat. "Good night, Thomas... Lily."

"Good night, Wayne," Lily's small voice said, the sound of it raising his heart beat.

He imagined that her cheeks would likely have reddened while saying good night, just as his felt. The awkwardness they had with each other seemed mutual. At times it seemed they were both uncertain how to respond or act around one another, but other times they were comfortable and even shared moments of joviality. Even though they'd known each other for less than a full day, there was already a sense of connection there, and being around her made Wayne feel protective of her, even if he hadn't promised her father that he would help their family, he'd still feel obligated to. He swallowed hard and remembered that day in front of the general store when he'd first seen her, and how even the way that she looked at him now didn't change. She made him feel human...and he'd spent so much time feeling less than human. Prison changed a man.

Perhaps losing his job at the ranch had been a blessing after all. If he'd never lost it, he wouldn't be here, now...he'd have never seen Lily again, because she would have left for Oregon without him. Perhaps even married someone else. And the thought of that twisted his stomach. He imagined all the different ways that the wrong man would have hurt Lily or her family and that made the protective feeling in him rise up again. No. As long as Wayne was charged with taking care of the Browne family, that was just what he was going to do. After a long moment of quiet from his upstairs neighbors, peppered with the song of crickets, Wayne finally succumbed to sleep.

CHAPTER 7

ABOUT 42 MILES FROM ALCOVE SPRINGS

A nother night had just about fallen on the camp, and the Browne family had already eaten supper. Wayne sat with them as Mr. Browne had a conversation with Mr. Cooper, the wagon master. At the other end of the log where he sat, Lily sat in front of the group campfire and let out a yawn. They'd been on the trail now for nearly ten days. Well over a hundred miles. But for the past two days they'd been sitting, waiting for the current at the Great Blue Earth River, as the natives called it, to settle down enough to ford because of the rain they'd had upstream making it run a bit too deep and too rapid to cross.

The days had been a bit tedious as they waited. Wayne had helped the cowboys keep the cattle and work animals fed and in a group so that they could keep better track of them. He'd even taken last watch each night to allow them to get more rest. In the meantime, Lily had grouped some of the camp's children together to work on teaching them some math and writing, but as games so that the children could learn without feeling restricted. They even made time for other games like "Duck, Duck, Goose" and "Hide and Seek," so the children weren't quite as bored as the adults. Still, she expressed that she really hoped that the morning would finally lead them to being allowed to cross.

He watched as she stifled another yawn, likely tired from a day of running around with the children. But apparently, Wayne wasn't the only one who noticed.

"If you're tired, Lily," her father said, "You can head back to the wagon for sleep. I'll keep an eye on Thomas until he's ready to join you."

Slowly she nodded and drew herself up to her feet.

Wayne frowned as she passed a little too close to the campfire. Then one of the other members of the train threw into the flames the fat from his meat to be burned off. The flames jumped as they consumed them and an errant spark leapt from the campfire and landed upon the hem at the back of Lily's calico dress.

Oblivious, Lily continued walking, fanning the ember until it sparked into a flame.

Leaping to his feet, Wayne watched in horror as the flames began to run up the dress, growing in size at a terrible rate. "Lily!" he yelled as he started toward her.

She looked back at him and then looked down in confusion just before her scream of terror pierced the air. Acting quickly, Wayne grabbed hold of the canvas blanket that some of the children had been sitting on earlier, thankful that no one had thought to pick it up yet. He rushed toward her and wrapped Lily in the heavy canvas blanket, frantically batting at the flames engulfing her dress. She fell to the ground.

"Lily!" Mr. Browne called out.

Panicked, she thrashed and kicked violently trying to escape the smothering blanket and the flames that likely burned her.

"It's okay, hold still!" Wayne urged her, but she continued fighting him in blind fright.

Her flailing foot kicked into Wayne's arm as he

wrestled to extinguish the last of the flames. He felt a crack and searing pain but held on until the fire was fully out.

Panting, Lily settled as she finally seemed to realize she was safe. Wayne gently unfurled the blanket revealing her ruined, charred dress. Worry gripped his throat. "Are you all right? Are you burned?

Still shaken, she shook her head and rubbed on her exposed leg. "No. I don't feel any pain. I... I think I'm all right."

Relieved, Wayne let out a slow breath, realizing that he was struggling to hold on to the blanket with his right hand. The arm felt strangely weak, and now that the heat of the moment was wearing off, he remembered the pain he'd felt there.

Lily gasped as she scrambled to her feet. "Your arm."

Her worried hands pulled the blanket from his and then touched the skin of his arm gently as she examined it. The arm bent unnaturally, almost as if he had a second elbow in the middle of it.

Frowning, he pulled away from her touch and tucked the arm against his chest. "It's not bad. I'm sure it will be fine."

"It will not," she declared with the angriest voice

he'd heard from her, though her eyes were already full of tears as she peered back up at him. "It's broken. I broke it, didn't I?"

He shrugged. "It doesn't hurt that bad."

She blinked and the tears ran down her cheeks. Now seeing her in that state actually hurt his heart more than his arm ached. She fixed him with a glare. "Stay here. I'll be right back."

After handing off the blanket to her father, who stood in the group that had formed around them, both him and Thomas looking pale and wide-eyed, the terror seeming too great for them, Lily rushed off in the direction of their wagon. The father and the boy followed after Lily. Several people in the group asked how he was, clapped him on the shoulder for thinking quickly, and confirmed with nods that, "Yep, it's definitely broken."

Even Wayne had to admit as he stood there waiting for Lily to return that the pain was beginning to settle in and there was definitely some throbbing from it. The crowd confirmed that there was no one in the camp who was a doctor though a couple of farmers came up, looking chagrined. The elder one with a red beard said, "If you'd like, my son and I can set the bone for you so that it will heal straight, but it's going to hurt quite a bit."

Wayne frowned, knowing that if he waited much longer the pain would be worse, so slowly, he nodded.

The younger farmer spit tobacco to the side and offered a bottle of whiskey. "A sip for courage and for the pain?" he asked.

"No, I'll be all right," Wayne said as he grit his teeth.

"Hold on," Lily said as she returned wearing a different dress and holding the burnt one in her hands along with a couple of sticks. She handed a smaller stick to Wayne. "Bite down on this so you don't injure your tongue."

He took it from her and did as she said. Then he offered his arm to the two farmers. One took hold of his elbow while the other grasped his hand and wrist. Then he looked up at Wayne. "You ready?"

Wayne nodded.

There was no counting to three. He wasn't even sure he'd done more than half a nod before the two farmers yanked on his arm in both directions. The searing pain that he felt this time was ten—no a hundred times worse than when it had been originally kicked. He groaned and spots crowded his vision. For a moment he felt woozy and was afraid that he might faint. He stumbled a step backwards when the two men released his arm.

Pain gripped his arm as though it were on fire past his elbow. He couldn't move it, and he didn't want to for fear of making the pain worse.

"I'm so sorry," Lily said as she approached again, tears still streaming down her face. "I... I can't believe I did this to you."

He shook his head as he took out the stick from between his teeth. "You were panicking. You didn't even know yourself. I can't imagine how it must have terrified you to be on fire."

A sob bubbled up and then in a hoarse whisper, she said, "My mother died in a fire."

His heart sank in his chest. "How horrifying."

She nodded. Then she took hold of the burnt dress that she held and tore off several strips. It was such a pretty brown and white dress with blue flowers dotted down the stripes. And it made Wayne sad that it had been ruined by the fire. With deft hands, Lily took hold of his arm and placed the sticks alongside of it and then used the strips from her dress to fashion a splint. Afterward, she also made a sling from the fabric and helped to tie it at the back of his neck.

"There," she said when the work had been completed. "I owe you my life now."

Frowning, he shook his head. "No, Lily. I just did what anyone else would have done."

"You're not just anyone, and no one else did. We were sitting in that crowd and no one thought as quickly or acted as fast as you did. I don't know how fast those flames would have grown. And when I saw the fire, my first instinct was to run. I wanted to run from the flames, hoping beyond hope that I could get away from them. My mind wasn't thinking clearly, but I know now that it only would have made things worse. And by then even you may not have been able to stop it with your blanket."

He shrugged. "You don't owe me anything," he said softly.

A small but sad smile tugged at her lip. "Still, I am here to help you. Tell me what you need, whatever it is and I will do it for you. And I suppose that I will need to step up and take care of the mules and oxen now that you're in a compromised position. It's a good thing you've already been teaching me how."

He scrunched his brow. That wasn't why he'd been teaching her how to take care of the animals. He'd been doing it because it allowed them to spend time alone together in a comfortable way, without any pressure of any kind and with them both being able to talk and interact with each other without awkwardness. The time that they'd been spending together had been a joy for him. He believed they were at least becoming friends. "I'm sure that this isn't going to hinder me that much."

With a tilt of her head, she shot a look of disapproval at him. "You think so? How many arms have you broken before?"

"None," he answered.

Her hands went on her hips as she stood akimbo. "I broke mine when I was seven. I used to have an affinity for climbing trees."

Somehow that both surprised Wayne, yet didn't surprise him.

"And as much as it hurts now, it's going to hurt like the dickens in the morning. And for the next few days it's going to throb and be so sore, you'll wonder if it will ever heal. Then in a week or so from now, it will start to feel better, but it will still be weak. Then your strength will start coming back in it a week or so after that, and you'll want to take it out of the splint and sling." She shook her finger at him as though admonishing him. "But I won't let you do that, you hear? It needs support in order to heal properly. And since this is your right arm, I will be there to help you wash up and feed you and whatever else you need help with."

He blinked at her, his eyes going wide.

When she met gazes with him, she realized all the intimate things that she was offering to do to help him, and her cheeks flushed a bright red and she shot her glance toward the ground quickly. "I... I mean I'll help you with what I can, and my father will help you with things that only another man can do. All right? That's settled." Quickly, she started marching away.

But she only made it about five steps before she turned back around. "Well, are you giving to stand there all night or are you coming?"

He couldn't help but huff a laugh as he cradled his arm to his chest and followed after his spitfire of a "wife."

Because she already had the page memorized, Lily continued speaking as she looked up from the book she was reading aloud to Thomas and studied Wayne's face while he sat nearby looking over at the cattle. It wasn't often that she saw Wayne's face with her spectacles on. The first time she did, she was surprised to find the scars that she saw there. He was younger than she thought he was. And there was a constant kindness and hurt in his hazel eyes that drew at her heartstrings. In a way, he kind of reminded her of a lost puppy she'd found when she was Thomas's age. She had cared for that puppy for almost three days when the owner had been found and it had been hard to give it up.

Was she starting to feel the same way about Wayne? Was he going to be difficult to give up when this journey was over? Her heart skipped a beat in her chest and her face flushed as she stuttered over a word and forgot her place in the book. Quickly she looked back down at the page, trying to smoothly pick it back up again.

"This is my sister's favorite story," Thomas said and then he turned to Wayne. "Have you read *The Count of Monte Cristo* before?"

Wayne turned his attention back to them and shook his head. "I'm afraid not. I've never heard this story before. I almost wish you had more time to read like this or could read faster so I could find out what happens next," he said with a warm smile.

It had been only three days since his arm had been broken. They'd had to wait another day before crossing the river and then it had been a little less than two days' travel to Alcove Springs, where they were resting for the remainder of the day to allow for bathing and cleaning clothes as well as filling their water barrels directly from the fresh water supply of the spring that came forth in a waterfall in the rocks. It was refreshing to take a little break, and this place was much nicer than the muddy bank by the Blue River crossing. Wayne had had to sit with her in the seat of the wagon with Bingo tied to the back of the cart instead of riding him since the injury. Lily peered over at him. "If you like, you can borrow the book and read ahead while you're resting that arm. Thomas would probably like it if you read aloud while we traveled."

His eyes went wide in shock for a moment and that sadness in them intensified as he shook his head. "No, I... I couldn't—um. I prefer when you read it. I don't want to ruin the story."

She frowned a little, feeling confused. "It's a book, so you're not making anything up. You couldn't ruin the story by changing the person reading it."

His eyes became pleading and even started looking a little panicked like a cornered animal. "I'm sure I could find a way to ruin it. I'd prefer if you were the one who kept on reading." And with that, he quickly stood and started off in the direction of the cattle and the cowboys.

"Why did he act like that?" Thomas asked. "For someone who couldn't wait to hear more of the story, he sure left in a hurry."

Lily studied him over her spectacles and wondered. Was it possible that Wayne was embarrassed about something? He behaved like it. She knew that some people didn't read aloud very well, and perhaps that was what the issue was. Regardless, she shrugged it off, but decided not to continue the story since she knew that Wayne wanted to hear it as well.

The next few days, the group started the journey on the stretch of trail they had to pass before reaching Fort Kearney. Mr. Cooper had told them they were about halfway to the Fort, but would need to travel an extra hour a day in order to ensure they made up for the days that they had spent waiting on the river crossings. It was amazing how much more tired they were traveling for eleven hours a day instead of ten. Lily had to admit that she liked the company of having Wayne sitting with her in the cart, although sometimes he'd spend part of the day walking alongside her father with the oxen pulling their larger wagon.

On that day, he was sitting with her in the cart as they were passing through a flat, sparse prairie. In the distance, Lily noticed a series of wooden stakes driven into the ground. As they drew closer, she could see worn letters carved into each stake. She squinted at them.

"Look, those stakes have messages on them," she said to Wayne. "I wonder who left them. Can you read what they say?"

Wayne shifted in his seat, glancing uncomfortably at the stakes. "Not sure. The words are too faded for me to read."

As they approached, Lily could squint and just make out what the stakes were warning against: "Beware of Sinkholes!" and "Ride Lightly!"

Puzzled, Lily asked "Did you see what that one said? We should be cautious since they warn of danger."

Looking ashamed, Wayne swallowed hard and shook his head. "I... didn't see. Truth is I never learned how to read. Only know my numbers and letters."

Lily was surprised but tried not to show it. "I see. Well, they warn of sinkholes in this area." She loosened her grip on the reins in her hands and turned to smile reassuringly. "I'd be happy to teach you to read, if you'd let me."

He turned and studied her, his brow furrowed. "Wouldn't that be too difficult? I hear it's hard for an adult to learn because they are more set in their ways than children."

She shrugged. "I'd be willing to try if you are. I am a schoolteacher after all. If you give up because someone says it's hard than you'll never try. And if you never try, then you'll never succeed, right?"

The confusion in his face wavered, and then softened, and became a smile. He shook his head. "I guess it's worth a try."

"Great! We'll start today. Next time we stop, I'll look for a book we can read."

"Actually," Wayne said as he leaned forward and pulled something from the back pocket of his dungarees. "I have this."

A small worn bible sat in his hand, the cover frayed and the pages bent in several directions. Lily wondered how long he'd had it and if it had some kind of special meaning to him. "That will work. You know your letters, right? Then look for the book of Proverbs, that will be a good place to start. It starts with a P and then a R."

After a moment of flipping through he came to a stop and said. "P.R.O.V...E.R...B.S?"

"That's the one," she said with a smile. "The first part says, 'The proverbs of Solomon the son of David, king of Israel; To know wisdom and instruction; to perceive the words of understanding; To receive the instruction of wisdom, justice, and judgment, and equity; To give subtilty to the simple, to the young man knowledge and discretion.'"

He stared at her a moment, wide-eyed. "How do you remember that?"

She smiled at him and shrugged. "I tend to remember everything I read. It's just the way I've always been. But, anyway... do you see how the word 'to' is repeated over and over. T. O. To. That's your first word. Look at it and recognize it. It's a small word that isn't telling you about a certain thing or even about an action. It just puts emphasis on other words. 'To.'"

"To," he said, slowly nodding. "T. O."

"Yes."

"What are the numbers here for?"

"Those are for people to use when they are referring to specific sayings or verses in the Bible. So, if I'm talking about Proverbs Chapter one, verse four, I'm specifically talking about..." she said looking over at his book and then pointing at the verse. "That one. Do you see?"

"To G.I.V.E"

"To give," she said.

"To give," he repeated and then he said it again.

"Now try to sound out the next word using your letters."

He swallowed hard studying it. "To give Ss...u... b...t... eh...L.T.Y"

She frowned, she didn't realize that was the next word and it was too hard for him. He gave it a good try but gave up on the last little bit. "It's all right," she reassured him. "It's subtilty. The B. is silent."

"Silent? Like you don't say it?"

"Right. How about the next word, it should be an easy one."

"To!" he said, a little excited and proud of himself.

She smiled so hard her cheeks were hurting. "That's right. T.O. To."

This was actually quite fun, and despite Wayne's fears that he wouldn't be a good student, he was enthusiastic and tried hard. It made Lily feel good that he'd opened up to her enough to admit that he wasn't able to read. This was a problem they could work on and solve together. Perhaps Wayne's broken arm had been a blessing after all, since it made it so that they had to sit together for hours on the wagon and spend time with one another. And with his learning to read, it would give Lily another goal to work toward. It was one of the reasons she'd become a teacher in the first place. There was hardly anything more satisfying than teaching someone something that they didn't know before. This was Wayne's chance to learn.

CHAPTER 8

ABOUT 100 MILES FROM JULESBURG

When they were about thirty or so miles past Fort Kearney, Lily looked west and didn't like the thunderheads brewing on the horizon. Dark ominous clouds rolled across the prairie, straight for them, and a call came out, "Whoa!"

She pulled the mule's reins and stopped them, but they pulled back against her, being unwilling to stop. The wind picked up and ripped through her bonnet, tugging at her hair and pulling half of it free. "Whoa," she called, throwing the word behind her and toward the next wagon in the hopes that the wind wouldn't pull the word away unheard.

"Circle up!" The wagon master called out, and

the wagons moved to form their normal circle just as thunder rolled from afar.

"What's going on?" Thomas asked, sticking his head out of the back of the wagon.

"Stay in the wagon." Lily still struggled against the stubborn mules that refused to listen to her.

Wayne came jogging around her father's wagon and rushed up to the mules, pulling on the reins from closer up with his good hand and stopping them, but they resisted him, too. His sharp gaze met with hers. "Grab the hobbles."

Lily reached in the back and grabbed the leather straps. Then she hopped down from the cart and rushed over with the hobbles. Thunder rolled through the clouds not far away. When she looked in that direction, she would swear the clouds were swirling. Her heart dropped into the pit of her stomach. "What are you doing?" she asked as he took the straps from her.

"We need to let the animals loose. If the storm hits and the animals are still harnessed to the wagon, they could do a lot of damage." He'd pulled his arm from the sling to attempt to place the hobbles on their legs.

"Give me that," Lily said as she yanked them from his hands. "You're still healing."

It had only been three weeks of healing on that arm, and it was bad enough that he'd not let her re-splint it the last few days. If he strained it too much, he'd break it again. But she heard Wayne grunt in response as he returned his arm to the sling and started undoing the harness straps with one hand. The moment she'd finished with hobbling the second mule, he pulled off one of the bridles, then the other. And the rain started. The mules hobbled away as quickly as the restrictions would let them, staying together and turning so their rear ends were toward the wind. Both of them lowered their heads pitifully. The rain poured in earnest, soaking Lily completely so that the hair that had broken free from her bonnet now stuck to her face. She swiped her eyes with her hand to see better and found Wayne heading to Bingo at the back of the cart. Groaning, she rushed to catch up with him and took the hobbles from him again. Just as they finished with loosing the horse from his tether, the thunder cracked deafeningly, directly overhead this time. And the rain suddenly had small ice balls in it.

"Lily! Take cover!" Wayne yelled as the ice balls became bigger and began pelting down violently.

People all around them in the train screamed and scrambled to take cover from the onslaught of tumbling ice chunks. The barrage beat against the wagon covers, threatening to rip through. A mule on the cart across from them in the circle reared up and fell over backwards as its hoof slipped in the mud. It crashed against the cart, splintering the wood.

The ice hit her back and shoulders hard causing distinct spots of sharp pain. Lilly grabbed hold of the back of the wagon and set a foot on the step, but her foot slipped and she slammed her body against the back of the cart and hit her head. Her other foot slipped, and she found herself sprawling in the mud and turning so that she landed on her back.

Hail continued to pelt against her as she cried out, trying to cover her face. She closed her eyes against the onslaught but as she did, the hail around her seemed to lighten. Opening her eyes and looking up, she found Wayne standing over top of her with his eyes intense. His back was bent, and his head tucked in under his arms which were propped against the wagon. His lips were pulled back in a grimace against the pain. "Can you crawl under the wagon?" he asked her gently.

She blinked up at him and nodded, and immediately scrambled to turn around and crawl under. After a moment, Wayne crawled under with her, and she realized that his arm was out of the sling again.

The jagged hailstones continued their onslaught for several minutes while the two of them watched from under the wagon. Lily prayed that Thomas was doing all right on his own in the cart and wondered if her father had made it out of the storm, too.

Finally, the hail tapered off, leaving the littered ice all over the ground almost like a strange sort of snow. Both she and Wayne breathed heavily under the wagon, neither of them moving or saying a word. There was only a drizzle of rain around them now, and the sun seemed to be breaking through as light surrounded them. People began to move about, and there was wailing.

Wayne grimaced as he attempted to crawl out from under the cart. Then he stood, and Lily crawled after him. He offered his good hand, holding his broken arm against his body, still outside of the sling. His arm was swollen and mottled with fresh bruises from the hail's strikes.

Lily's eyes welled with tears upon seeing Wayne's new injuries. Despite his compromised arm, he had selflessly risked more harm to protect her and the animals and their cart.

Wayne looked away and winced, then he attempted to smile. "See, the animals didn't go very far. They just needed to adjust themselves so that they didn't take on too much damage during the storm."

She nodded, even though she didn't see the mules or the horse, or her father's oxen. All she could see was the man who stood in front of her, covered in mud and his red, swollen arm. She shook her head and swiped at her tears and then stepped forward and gingerly took hold of the arm. "Is it rebroken?"

He grunted and winced where she touched it. "It smarts, but I don't think it's rebroken. Just bruised."

"Let me splint it again, just to be sure," she said, looking up at him, ready to insist if he resisted.

But he only nodded.

She grabbed the back of the wagon and set her foot on the step, deeper this time in hopes that she wouldn't slip again. When Lily pulled herself up, she was relieved to see Thomas looking up at her. "Are you okay?" she asked him immediately as she pulled herself the rest of the way into the cart.

His eyes were wide and welling with tears, but he nodded, the blanket still wrapped around his body and his hair messed up. "I just put myself under the blanket when it was hitting the roof. Where were you? I was so scared."

She crawled over to him and pulled him into an

embrace. "I'm sorry. I fell and couldn't get up into the cart with you. But Wayne helped me and we both crawled under the wagon instead."

"So, you were right under me the whole time?" He pulled back and looked up at her.

"Yes," she said nodding and smoothing down his dark blond hair. "Now I need to get the sticks and cloth that I washed in the river yesterday. Can you hand them to me?"

He nodded and reached behind him for the items she asked for. As he handed them to her, he asked, "Is Wayne going to let you splint it again?"

"He has no choice this time. I'll do it whether he wants it or not." She took the items and started crawling back toward the exit of the cart on her knees.

"Do you love him, sister?" Thomas's small voice asked, making her freeze where she was as butter-flies flitted in her stomach.

She turned around and pinned her brother with her gaze and frowned. "What makes you ask a thing like that?"

He shrugged, "You take care of him. He takes care of you. Sometimes I see you look at each other the way that Mother and Father used to when they were in a good mood."

Shaking her head, she huffed a laugh. "Well, we've hardly known each other more than a month. We're just becoming friends."

"Oh... All right," her brother said with a shrug.

For a moment, Lily just looked at her brother, wondering what could have possessed him to ask such a thing. Surely her brother was just mistaken. He couldn't really understand the ways of adults at only nine years old. She shook her head again and continued to the back of the cart, preparing herself to redress Wayne's battered limb. No, what she felt now wasn't love, was it? It was affection for her friend. It was gratitude for Wayne's continued protection and help. It was guilt because it was her fault that he'd been injured in the first place, and her fault again that he was hurting again that day. Not love. Just... what? What was this feeling she had for him called?

With a deep breath to steel herself, she reached up and pulled herself out of the cart.

Finally, the day came when Wayne could rid himself of the wretched sling. It had been a full month since he'd injured it again in the hail storm, and Lily had been on him like a hawk, making sure that he'd kept it splinted for two weeks afterward, and that he'd kept it in the sling for a full two weeks more. She'd been much more lenient from the time of the break, but after the storm, she didn't budge an inch. That morning, at breakfast, Lily had looked over his arm as keenly as a doctor would have, bending his wrist and elbow and asking if any of the motions that she was making hurt him. When he answered, honestly, that it did not, she succumbed with a sigh that he could go without the sling, but to continue to be careful with the arm. He agreed with a wide grin. And took off like a shot to go get back on his gelding. Now that he was free of the wretched sling, he could regain total freedom by sitting on the back of his horse and even helping move the cattle herd that was pushed along with the train to keep them all fed.

The stretch of land to Independence Rock was almost entirely red clay and desert with sparse grasses here and there, so there wasn't much for the cattle or the work animals to feed on. They'd taken to feeding them the grain they'd gotten from Fort Laramie but they had to be careful not to let the animals consume too much at once to avoid sickness and running out of grain before they reached the

Green River Valley where they'd find good grazing again. But that was over three hundred miles of terrain they'd need to traverse before then.

Right now, Wayne was feeling giddy. He'd discovered a few weeks ago, from Mr. Browne, that Lily's birthday was on Independence Day... how fitting it would have been if they'd reached Independence Rock by then, but they were still a day or so away from it. Regardless, Wayne had arranged for a gift. The wagon master was a horseman, so he'd brought extra horses for keeping the cattle and for hunting parties and other uses and had them tethered to a few of the carts that were used by the wagon master and the cook. Wayne had arranged to buy one of the horses for Lily. He had worked with the cook doing odd jobs—carrying water buckets with his good arm, acting as butcher's assistant when the cook was cutting meat and hides, Wayne carried the slop bucket out to the grazing area when the cook peeled vegetables, and though it took him a while, he'd even done dishes after the meals. Even the odd jobs Wayne had done, he'd done them in secret so that Lily wouldn't ask what he was doing. But it had all been worth it, since he was able to buy the little gray cow pony mare and a saddle for her as well. Wayne knew that he had to continue working with the cook even though his arm had healed in order to pay off the debt entirely, but he was just happy that he was able to give Lily her gift that day.

When he met up with Mr. Cooper after breakfast, the man met him with a hearty handshake. "So, I see that your sling is gone. Does that mean that your nurse-wife has now given you leave of it with a clean bill of health?"

Heat rushed to his cheeks at the thought of Lily as his nurse-wife. He swallowed hard before answering with a grin. "Yes, she has. That means we're ready to go ride today. Will Bob be able to drive the oxen for Mr. Browne so that he can drive the mules for me?"

"Yep. Bob has already talked to Mr. Browne," Mr. Cooper said and then leaned in and whispered, "In secret, of course."

"Thank you, sir."

"Not at all. Not at all." Mr. Cooper waved a hand in front of his face. "The mare is saddled and ready for you. Here comes Bob with her now."

Young Bob, Mr. Cooper's son led the mare toward them by the reins. The mare's silver mane sparkled in the morning sunlight. She really was a pretty thing, and when Wayne had chosen her, it was because the mare had reminded him of Lily. "Perfect," was all he could manage.

"Now, all we have are stock saddles. I hope your young lady doesn't usually ride sideways," Mr. Cooper said with a chuckle.

The blood drained from Wayne's face. He hadn't thought of that. What if Lily rejected his gift because she wasn't able to ride astride a horse like men did. How was this going to work?

Mr. Cooper clapped him on the shoulder. "I was just kidding you, son. I'm sure she'll be fine." He gave Wayne a little shove toward the mare.

Bob handed him the reins with a smile. "Have fun."

"Thank you," Wayne said as he took them and patted the mare on the forehead. Then he looked up at Mr. Cooper. "Thank you both for making this happen today."

Both of them nodded. "You're welcome," they said almost simultaneously, making it apparent with their similar smiles that they were father and son.

Wayne swallowed down the knot that was rising up in his throat as butterflies danced in his stomach. He knew that his plan was a good one, and that his gift was perfect, but now that he was ready to offer them to Lily, he wondered if she would like them.

What if she didn't? Questions rose up in his mind while he walked with the mare down the row of wagons toward the two that were owned by the Browne family. Then he caught sight of Lily standing with her father by their mules, tying on her bonnet, and his nervousness was replaced by excitement again. The sunlight played in her gold hair and shined just as well as a newly minted coin. Her eyes were drawn to him as he approached.

Her brow furrowed, and she tilted her head when he drew closer. "That's not Bingo," she said and then looked to the back of the wagon where Bingo was tethered. "Is the gelding all right?"

Wayne smiled. "He's fine. This isn't Bingo—it's Lacy. Want to meet her?"

Lily's eyes sparkled with excitement as she approached the mare and let the horse sniff her hands then she rubbed her fingers through the hair on the mare's forehead. "You're a pretty one, aren't you Lacy. Yes you are."

"You like her?" Wayne asked, his excitement and nervousness wrestling in his stomach.

"I do. She's very pretty."

"She's yours," he finally said.

Lily stopped, blinked and then looked up at him, confused.

121

"Happy birthday," he said.

Immediately, her eyes went wide. She gasped. "How did you know?"

"Your father happened to mention it a few weeks ago."

She shook her head, still rubbing the mare's forelock. "This is too much though. You bought me a horse? No. She's just borrowed, right?"

"Not borrowed. Yours."

For a long moment, Lily just looked at the mare seeming to try to get it to sink in. Finally, she looked up at him with misty eyes. "Thank you."

"There's more," he said just as Mr. Browne and Thomas approached. "Mr. Cooper's son, Bob, is going to drive your father's wagon so that your father can drive the mule cart."

She looked at her father with a questioning glance. And the gentleman nodded with a smile. Her gaze returned to Wayne. "Why?"

"We're about forty miles or so from Independence Rock, but Mr. Cooper tells me there's a hill where you can catch sight of the rock from miles out. Since it's Independence Day...and your birthday, I thought it might be fitting for us to ride out ahead of the train and get a view of the rock, since we won't be able to see it today otherwise."

Her eyes widened and she looked again toward her father before returning her gaze to Wayne. "Really?"

He nodded and gestured toward the stock saddle. "That is, unless you can't ride astride."

Laughter—pure and angelic and like a bell—filled the air. Lily immediately stepped over and shoved a foot in the stirrup. Wrapping her long skirt around her legs, she mounted and used the cloth to form a sort of dungarees. Then she reined the horse toward the back of the cart. With an excited smile, she said, "Let's go get Bingo and ride!"

CHAPTER 9

ABOUT 100 MILES PAST FORT LARAMIE

As they reached the summit of the hill, it was late in the afternoon and the sun was getting low on the horizon. Lilly drew in a deep, satisfied breath. "There it is," she said as she spotted the large, round monolith in the distance, known as Independence Rock.

Wayne nodded, but his gaze was cast toward the side of the hill where four mounds of rocks and dirt marked makeshift graves. Lily's heart dropped as she spotted them. They didn't look very old. Likely the wagon train ahead of them had buried members of their train. Originally, their wagon train had thirty-two wagons a part of the journey, but at Fort

Laramie, they had three turn back. They'd lost a man in the hailstorm whose oxen had destroyed their wagon and trampled them, and a child to fever, but it seemed they'd been fortunate so far to have only lost two.

Stepping forward and blocking her sight of the graves, Wayne gestured toward the view ahead of them. "I think the ride was worth it to see Independence rock on Independence Day, don't you?"

Her smile returned as she pushed those morbid thoughts out of her mind. "And my birthday."

"And your birthday."

Truth was that she'd smiled so much on the ride there that her cheeks ached. It wasn't just getting a chance to see the rock. It was being able to get away from the monotony of driving the mules. Getting to ride a horse for the first time in a long while. Even just spending this time alone with Wayne, who had grown to be a close friend. "How far ahead do you imagine we are?"

He shrugged. "Mr. Cooper said that we'd probably reach this summit with the wagon train at about midday tomorrow, so that means that they'll make camp about ten miles out or so. It will probably take us about an hour and a half to get back there and meet up with them. If we just walk."

"Who wants to just walk though?" She laughed and reined her horse back down the trail the way they came and started trotting.

Wayne rode up beside her and said, "If we go too fast, the train won't have reached their camp yet."

"That'll be fine." She continued posting the trot in the stock saddle, even though it felt a bit wider than the English saddles she was used to.

"All right, then," he said as he started to lope ahead.

"Unfair!" she squeezed her calves and asked Lacy to catch up.

For several minutes the two of them just loped together, feeling the movements of their horses' legs under them and the wind threatening to pull the bonnet from Lily's head. Then they pulled the horses back down to the walk to allow them to rest as they continued on the trail. Through the low parts of the trail, where the mud had been, they could see deep ruts created by wagon wheels. And occasionally, a hoof print left by an ox drew Lily's attention. Large rocks dotted the plain beside the trail and since they were nearing the river, sparse grass rose in browns and greens through the sandy soil. Occasionally, Lacy would reach down and snatch a bite of grass as they went along, and Lily would let her, but wouldn't let the mare stop entirely to get her fill. Still, Lacy's occasional stopping was allowing Wayne and Bingo to get ahead a little ways on the trail.

Without warning, a rattlesnake slithered onto the trail, spooking Wayne's bay gelding. Before Wayne could react, Bingo reared up violently with a panicked whinny, flinging Wayne from the saddle. Lily watched in horror as Wayne landed with a sickening thud. He lay motionless as his frenzied horse charged off, one boot stuck in the stirrup, dragging Wayne's limp body along.

Immediately, Lucy jigged in place, ready to run in a panic with her companion. Heart plunging, Lily released the reins and kicked her horse forward, desperately chasing the runaway steed as Wayne bounced violently behind. If his foot stayed stuck, he could be trampled or dragged to death across the sharp rocks. She rode hard, focused on catching the horse before it reached the patch of prickly cacti ahead.

Lily finally overtook the frantic animal just before the cactus patch. Grabbing the loose reins, she pulled with all her might, bringing him to a precarious halt. Throwing herself from the saddle as she dismounted, she rushed to Wayne's broken, bleeding body, praying she wasn't too late. She twisted his foot from the stirrup and then turned toward him.

With shaky hands, Lily examined Wayne's still form. Through his tattered clothes she saw painful scrapes and bruises but no life-threatening gashes. Inwardly, she thanked God and sighed in relief that the injuries seemed relatively minor though he was still unconscious.

Quickly she stood and returned to Lacy, who stood with Bingo—his sides heaving with heavy breaths as he continued to pant. After grabbing her canteen, Lily returned to Wayne and gently splashed water on his face. He stirred faintly and groaned, his eyes slowly blinking open. Lily exhaled, overjoyed to see him conscious again.

"Wayne! Can you hear me?" she asked anxiously.

He winced and nodded slightly before grimacing in pain. "What...happened?" he rasped.

Lily quickly explained about the rattlesnake spooking his horse and his traumatic drag through the rocks. Tears pricked her eyes remembering the terror of seeing his limp body flung about.

Though battered and dazed, Wayne struggled to sit up. Lily helped support him. "Just lie still, you need to rest," she urged him.

"I'll be...alright," Wayne insisted hoarsely. He

tentatively moved his limbs, assessing the damage. "Though I ache terribly, nothing seems broken this time."

Shaking her head at him as he smiled up at her, she held him by the elbow and shoulder. "Let me help you up."

Nodding, he scrambled to get his legs under him before he stood. Once she released him, he put a hand to his back. "Ugh. That smarts."

"You've got quite a few scrapes there and they are filled with gravel and dirt. If you'd like, I can clean them up as much as I can with my canteen." She lifted the flask in her hand.

He nodded, and then immediately removed his shirt.

Lily's heart skipped a beat, and she nearly gasped. Immediately she cast her gaze to the ground. Wayne was much more muscular than she realized. When he turned around, she lifted her eyes and stepped closer, trying to keep her mind on the task of cleaning the cuts instead of his manly scent or the fact that his skin felt soft under her touch. She poured the water onto his back and gingerly took out rocks with her fingernails.

Wayne winced a few times, sucking in a breath, but was staying still under her gentle touch. Lily kept working at it until the cuts were as clean as she could make them with the water alone. "There," she said after several minutes. "Done."

With a look of relief on his face Wayne pulled the shirt back over his head with a groan and then shoved his arms through the sleeves as he turned around and pulled it down, but not before flashing his manly chest at Lily once more. Her hands gripped the canteen tightly as her cheeks flushed and she found herself examining the rocks on the ground again.

"I think I'm going to be mighty sore for the next day or two, but at least it doesn't seem that I broke my arm again."

Lily nodded, still not ready to look up at him with her cheeks flushed.

Wayne didn't seem to notice, though as he stepped over to Bingo and patted the gelding on the neck and then he leaned down and checked the horse's legs. "It doesn't look like there's a snakebite or any injuries. I think he'll ride fine if you're ready to get back on?"

Letting out a slow breath and feeling a bit more like herself, Lily looked up and nodded. "I'm ready."

In one smooth motion, Wayne mounted his gelding. Because Lily felt a bit weak in the knees, she was glad that Lacy wasn't as tall as Bingo. She stepped up to the mare and put a foot in the stirrup and then pulled herself back up into the stock saddle. With a deep breath, Wayne slumped a bit in the saddle and then started walking back toward where the wagon train was going to camp for the night.

Lily nudged her little mare forward and followed after Wayne. Her pony's stride wasn't quite as big as Bingo's so she tended to keep pace a few steps behind them. Occasionally, Wayne would stop to allow them to catch up. After a short bit of awkward silence, Lily started the conversation again. "I hadn't seen many snakes on the trail until today."

"Well, you've been mostly staying with the train. With that many people and animals around, snakes tend to make themselves scarce. They aren't itching for a fight any more than we are."

"That makes sense." Lily rested the hand she held the reins with on the pommel of the saddle.

"When you're off with a hunting party or working the cattle you'll see snakes more often because everybody's not so tightly packed together."

Lily nodded and relaxed a bit more into her saddle. The light and fun conversation they'd had before was gone with the sobriety of the moment, but the quiet easy rhythm that they'd found just by being together was becoming something that Lily was growing accustomed to. Sitting next to him on the trail in saddles wasn't much different than sitting next to him on the bench of the wagon seat. The two of them were true friends, and she hoped that even after they got their annulment in Oregon at the end of the journey, they could continue in their friendship because if he just left—if she never saw him again... well, she really didn't want to consider that possibility.

CHAPTER 10

ABOUT 50 MILES PAST FORT BOISE

"What was that?" Lily put down the book she'd been reading aloud to Wayne and Thomas and looked to the back of the train.

"Gunfire," Wayne said with a frown and handed the reins of the mules over to Lily and then called out as he stood from the seat, "Whoa."

Other calls of "Whoa" came at about the same time from in front and behind them. As soon as Lily pulled the reins on the mules, Wayne leapt from the wagon seat.

"What's going on?" Thomas asked, climbing out from the back of the wagon and into the seat beside Lily.

She frowned. "I'm not sure."

Another gunshot. Then two more. Fear gripped Lily's heart as they sounded closer this time. She looked for Wayne and found him already mounted on Bingo and tearing off in the direction of the gunfire with a rifle in his free hand.

"Get back into the back of the wagon and hand me the shotgun," she commanded her brother, and Thomas immediately climbed back over the seat and handed her the weapon. She loaded it quickly.

They were two and a half days journey outside of Fort Boise in September, and though they hadn't gone more than about thirty miles due to the uphill trek, they were just far enough from the fort that getting help from them would be near impossible.

Her father came running up just as she climbed down from the wagon. "No, Lilly," he called out as he approached. "Get in the wagon and lie down. It's too dangerous."

Just as she was about to protest, more gunfire and a rider came galloping up beside the train. He wore a darker hat than she recalled anyone in their party wearing and a bandana covered part of his face. She lifted the shotgun but her finger hesitated before touching the trigger. With a shotgun, she was a decent shot, but could she really do it? Could she really kill a man?

"Give me that." Her father yanked the weapon from her hands. "Now get in the cart like I told you."

Feeling admonished by her father, she rushed to climb up into the seat and over the back of the cart. The loud report of the shot gun thundered through the air and shook her to the core. Thomas peeked from under the blanket. "Thank goodness you're here," he said.

She nodded to him and lay down with him just as more gunfire rang out and the pounding of hooves, shouts, and all manner of commotion followed. Was her father really going to be all right out there? Would Wayne, who rode off toward danger? *Lord, please let them be safe*, she prayed. Then she started to feel wet, and panicked. Was it blood? Was she shot? No, she'd felt no pain anywhere. Was Thomas injured? Now the trepidation gripped her heart in an icy hold. Immediately she sat up, needing to check if Thomas was all right. *Oh, please let him be all right.*

Outside, the commotion continued but it had been a full minute since the last gunshot. It had to be safe enough now. She lifted the blanket and found a lot more wetness, but no blood. Then she realized that their water barrel was leaking. Gasping, she rushed over to it, shoved her thumb over the hole and frantically looked to find something to plug it with. To think that a bullet had gotten so close to her and Thomas, and that it struck the barrel. She shook her head at the fear she felt gripping her heart. Then her eyes fixed on the bar of glycerine soap sitting in a towel. "Thomas, grab that bar of soap and shave me a small square of it to plug this hole, about a half inch."

Nodding, her brother pulled out his pocket knife and made his way to the towel that held their soap and cut a small square off the corner. It was a little bigger than she likely needed, but it would have to do. After withdrawing her thumb from the hole, she shoved the soap into it, twisting the glycerin to make it fit. Pieces of the soap curled to both sides of the plug and there was some slipperiness around it where the soap had dissolved a bit in the water, but it looked like it would hold, albeit temporarily.

"Looks like it's over," Thomas said from where he stood in the cart, leaning over the seat and looking out.

She sucked her teeth. "Get down from there."

"But Father is just standing around with Mr. Cooper and some other men. There's a bandit at their feet. Looks like they might have killed someone."

Her heart sank to her stomach. Was her father the one who killed the bandit? Would she have been the one to kill him if she'd pulled that trigger before her father yanked the gun away? "I said, get down, Thomas. Now. It's not safe regardless."

Ignoring her, he continued to inform her of what was going on. "Looks like Wayne is back, too."

Relief washed over her, and tears stung the backs of her eyes. She hadn't realized how worried she was that Wayne would be hurt until that moment. After shuffling closer, she pulled herself to her feet and rubbed the top of Thomas's head. "That's enough. Now I mean it. Get down."

"Aw shucks," he said with disappointment as he sat back down into the cart.

"You can start cleaning up that mess with a towel, too."

"Fine," he huffed.

Wisps of hair had made their way out of Lily's bonnet, so she pulled it from her head, straightened her hair as best she could without a mirror and then tied the bonnet again. Then she climbed over the seat and hopped down from the cart.

"Lily! You should get back in that cart where it's safe," her father immediately commanded.

Ignoring her father this time, she went straight to Wayne, who stood next to Bingo. "Are you all right? What happened?"

Brow furrowed, he looked down at her. "The bandits had rustled all the cattle and killed two of the cowboys. They were outnumbered. There were twelve bandits. If I had been there, helping them..."

"Then you would have been hurt or possibly killed, too," Lily said with a frown.

He shook his head. "You don't understand, Lily. I was supposed to be there today, but I asked Caleb to take my place so that I could sit with you and with Thomas and read. Now Caleb's gone. It shouldn't have been like that."

Her heart ripped in her chest as she felt genuine pain there at the thought that the man who'd replaced Wayne had died. She felt horrible that Caleb was gone, but also glad that it wasn't Wayne. And the guilt intermingled with the sadness she harbored there. "Maybe not, but I'm still glad that you're all right."

The sadness in his eyes was evident, he was distraught, and Lily felt the need to comfort him. For once, she didn't fight it and reached forward, pulling

Wayne into an embrace. He stiffened under her touch for a half a moment, but then softened and his arms wrapped around her, too. For a long moment, Lily just held Wayne tightly, refusing to let him go. On the top of her head, she felt his cheek rest. Her ear rested against his chest, and she could hear his heart thundering so fast, equal to her own. His warmth was addicting. She could stay there forever if he'd allow it. If time would only stand still. Tears fell down her cheeks. Tears for the man who'd died instead of Wayne. Tears of guilt for the way she was glad it was him instead. Tears for the fact that time wouldn't stand still and she needed to let go of her friend. Slowly, she loosened her grip on him and stepped back, swiping the tears from her cheeks

Looking down at her gently, Wayne also had tears on his cheeks and his bottom lids were red. His hands remained on her waist. They stood there with each other, close enough that their breath intermingled and just felt all their sadness but also their comfort with each other.

Then her father cleared his throat from behind her and broke the spell they were under. Wayne released her and stepped back, his cheeks reddening a bit. She felt heat flush into her own as she also turned away from Wayne, feeling like the moment they'd had was precious, but stolen. Her father placed a hand on her shoulder. "Both you and Thomas are all right?"

She nodded. "They put a hole in our water barrel, though. I pushed some soap in the hole for now, but we need to find a suitable plug."

"I'm sure the cook has a cork that we can whittle down to the right size," Mr. Cooper offered, and that was when Lily realized that there'd been a whole crowd of people around her and Wayne when they'd hugged.

More heat went into her cheeks, and she cast her gaze down. "I should go ask him."

"No, I'll do it," Wayne offered, and she peered up just to see him spin on his heel and lead Bingo to the back of the cart.

She couldn't help but feel a tug of sadness in her gut as she watched him go.

CHAPTER 11

After they'd assessed the damage from the bandits, they found that they had lost a total of four lives from the wagon train. Wayne had helped Bob and Mr. Cooper dig holes for the bodies. Then they measured their resources and found they were dangerously low on meat but had enough hardtack that they should be able to make it if they found good hunting. With that news, and due to their losses, some of the wagons turned back for Fort Boise, but nineteen wagons, including the Browne family, decided to continue on.

It was a difficult, slow-going trek uphill through the Blue Mountains. Morning haze surrounded them til almost noon each morning. Snow fell in gentle flurries every other day as they neared the top of the mountain, and they trudged through mud and snow only to make it about ten miles or so a day. The trail which had been fairly easy up to that point became much more difficult.

The Browne family was dangerously low on water due to their compromised barrel and the soap that had made them throw out the remainder in that barrel before they found a cork to repair it. They portioned it out so that they drank only a little each day with hopes that they'd make it until they found a water source that would allow them to refill their two barrels. They'd asked if anyone had any to spare, but were turned down as everyone was short on the amount of water needed. Especially since they were eating hardtack.

Each day, Wayne joined the hunters, but they often came back empty-handed or with a rabbit or squirrel or two, which was barely enough to season a pot of stew. And the cook was running low on potatoes as well. Things were coming apart at the seams. Each morning, Wayne was waking hungry, and he went to bed with his mouth dry and stomach gnawing at him, and it had been that way for more than a week now.

If they could get a real snow, they'd at least have the chance of collecting it, but the dusting that they had on the ground was only enough to create mud when they trudged their way through it. What made matters worse were that Lily and Mr. Browne were giving up portions of their rations for Thomas's sake. The child was top priority, since they didn't want him to suffer considering his health. Though the boy seemed to be doing better on the trip than most, Wayne thought, but he could understand the fear that ate at both of them that Thomas could make a turn for the worse at any moment. And still the trail went on ahead of them.

"Whoa," a call went out from the front.

"Whoa," Wayne immediately repeated, and he heard the cries of several others down the row of wagons.

Lily cast him a questioning glance, and he nodded back to her. The reading and comfortable conversation that they used to have while traveling had grown quieter than the grumbling of their own bellies. But right now, it was midday—much too early to be considering setting up camp. So, he reined Bingo toward the front of the wagons and picked up a trot to reach Mr. Cooper to ask what was going on. But as he drew closer to the front, he saw two new wagons grouped together, missing oxen or mules to carry them forward. Six people stood with the wagons—four men, a woman and a young boy about Thomas's age, who hid behind his mother's skirt.

Mr. Cooper hopped down from his wagon at about the same time as Wayne rode up and dismounted.

"Hello!" The older gentleman called out to him. "I'm John Avery. We are more than happy to see you and your train. We've been stranded here for two days, as we set up camp with another train, but they abandoned us and stole our mules."

Wayne frowned. Their story was horrible, making him wonder how the train could decide to do such a horrible thing.

"I see," said Mr. Cooper. "We can spare mules and oxen to help you all out, but will you continue on the trail with us for Fort Nez Perce or head back for Fort Boise?"

"We'd like to join your train, if you don't mind."

Mr. Cooper nodded. "Do you happen to have any rations? We're a bit low if we're taking on more mouths to feed."

A wide grin spread across Mr. Avery's face. "God has been with us on the hunt. We've got a couple hundred pounds of venison and fresh flour. We have goods to spare."

"And water?" Mr. Cooper asked.

"There's a mountain spring about a half hour's hike from here. We can show you where," Mr. Avery answered.

For the first time in the last few days, Wayne felt a spark of hope in his chest. Maybe this was just the blessing that they were waiting for. The men with the new wagons seemed friendly, as did the woman, but the young boy had yet to show his face as he sniffled and clung to his mother.

MEASLES. THE VERY PEOPLE WHO BROUGHT WITH them hope of overcoming the shortages of food and water that the wagon train had been suffering from also brought with them a terrible sickness. Wayne had wondered why they'd been left and abandoned by the previous wagon train, but it wasn't even two days later that their train discovered the reason.

And by then, it was too late.

Almost immediately it started spreading through the camp like wildfire. And both Wayne and Mr. Browne were among the first to contract it. They both kept distance from Lily and Thomas, in the hopes that they wouldn't pick up the disease, as

Thomas was already sick with one illness and didn't need another that could possibly kill him.

The food and water had been a blessing that allowed everyone to continue the journey, but it was even slower going downhill than Wayne had imagined since the incline was much steeper than it had been going uphill. Instead of pulling the wagons, the oxen and mules braced against the weight to keep the wagons from careening down the mountainside. It was a treacherous journey. And they needed rest more often since nearly half of the camp had contracted the measles.

Wayne coughed, riding beside Mr. Browne's wagon, but he rode a bit farther to the back and side so he could keep an eye on Lily's wagon to make sure she didn't need any help. His eyes watered and nose ran, and the blasted rash on his back and shoulders drove him crazy with wanting to scratch.

But he knew better. It wasn't going to help, and it would only make the disease more transmissible. Mr. Cooper said their best defense against the disease was to keep things as clean as possible, to not touch each other and keep their distance. So, no more gathering by the campfire in the evenings. Each wagon had to have their own camp, and Lily had even taken to making her own meals with Thomas.

From his position walking next to the wagon, Mr. Browne coughed. Because he and Mr. Avery had both been bankers so they'd become fast friends and spent a great deal of time together. And that was how Mr. Browne contracted the disease first. What scared Mr. Browne the most was that yesterday, they'd had to bury Mr. Avery's son, Sylvester. Even now as he walked next to his oxen, Mr. Browne seemed to be in a wide-eyed daze, pale, and feverish looking. Then as Wayne was watching, Mr. Browne stumbled and fell forward onto his face.

"Whoa!" Wayne immediately cried out. He could only thank God that they weren't currently on one of the steeper sections of the downhill slope so that stopping was actually possible. He jumped from his horse as he heard the continued shouts of "Whoa" down the train and pulled the oxen to a halt.

His heart sinking to his stomach, he rushed to Mr. Browne's side. The man hadn't even attempted to stand or turn over, and that made Wayne worry even more. When he turned the older gentleman over, he found the man wincing, eyes closed, sweat beading on his pale forehead and tears streaming down his face. "Mr. Browne? Are you all right?"

The man cracked open his sore-looking, red eyes. "So tired," he croaked, his voice hoarse and strangled.

Unfortunately, Wayne could understand how his friend felt. "It's early, but I'll go see if Mr. Cooper is all right with setting up camp here. Do you think you could stand?"

"I don't know, son. I don't have any strength left."

A feminine voice asked, "What's going on?" It was Lily, keeping her distance at the back of the ox wagon.

"Tell her to stay away," the hoarse voice asked.

"Keep back," Wayne called out, but his own voice croaked and a sharp pain struck his throat in his attempt to raise it.

"I will. But... but is Father all right?"

"Tell her that I'm fine."

Wayne frowned. It would be a lie to tell Lily that. She'd hate him if something happened to Mr. Browne and Wayne had lied to her about it. He couldn't do it. Instead he met gazes with Lily and shook his head.

A sob bubbled up from her as she covered her face with her hands and then crouched down where she stood, obviously wanting to come closer but fearing to. Wayne's heart shattered to pieces in his chest for her. He wanted to comfort her, to embrace her, like she had done when Caleb had passed, but that would be worse than her coming closer to see to her father. No, Wayne couldn't do that and would suffer from a distance the way he needed to.

"Mr. Browne?" Mr. Cooper asked from the other side of Wayne. "Do we need to stop and set camp? Can you stand?"

"We need to stop," Wayne said past the lump that had formed in his throat. "Mr. Browne needs to rest."

Mr. Browne gripped Wayne's shirt sleeve weakly, suddenly looking even more pale. His eyes were barely open in slits. "I can't... I don't think I'm going to be able to stand. I need... I need you to promise me, Wayne. Promise me you'll take care of Lily and Thomas."

"No, sir. You can't give up. You need to get up for their sakes. You need to push down deep and stand up and fight this sickness. Can't you do that? For Thomas and Lily?"

Mr. Browne's weak hold on Wayne's shirt released and his hand fell away. "I gave all I could just to put one foot in front of the other for as long as I could. I'm finished—I know that I am. I can feel my heart pounding in my chest. It's beating faster than I've ever felt before. I have no strength left."

"Surely you're wrong, sir."

"Let's try to get him to his feet," Mr. Cooper said, coming closer. The wagon master had been keeping his distance from the sick as well, but he immediately came over to help Mr. Browne up. His hand gripped Mr. Browne's shoulder.

Together, Mr. Cooper and Wayne lifted Mr. Browne up to his feet, but the man just leaned upon them and his knees continued to buckle, unable to hold his own weight. It wasn't til then that Wayne realized how much weight the man had lost. The once almost portly man now had bones sticking out in every possible way. It saddened Wayne.

The older man coughed and shook his head. "I'm finished. Promise me, Wayne. I need to hear you say it."

The sobs continued behind the men and grew louder. There was nothing that Lily could do, but Wayne understood that she just wanted to be allowed to come closer at a time like this. She was mourning her father even though he wasn't dead yet. Adamantly, Wayne answered. "No, sir. You need to live."

This time, a sob escaped Mr. Browne. "Even if I live, son, promise me. Please."

Frowning, Wayne couldn't hold out any longer. He didn't want for Mr. Browne to give up, but he also didn't want for the man to suffer in pain and feel as if Wayne didn't care. "You'll live, sir. You have to. And even as you live, I will still take care of Lily and Thomas."

Relief softened the features of Mr. Browne's face as he slumped in their arms. But the man didn't take another breath and didn't lift his head again. No, this was exactly what Wayne didn't want. He shouldn't have promised what he did. He shook the man. "Mr. Browne. No. Please don't. Mr. Browne?"

Mr. Cooper set a hand on Wayne's shoulder. "He's gone, son."

"No. He can't be," Wayne whispered, his throat closing on him as tears blurred his vision.

"He is. And you didn't do this with your promise, son. He would have died either way, and it's better that you let him die in peace, knowing that you'll take care of what's most precious to him. He was leaving and didn't want them to be abandoned. You only promised that they wouldn't be. All right?"

Even though in his mind Wayne knew that Mr. Cooper was right, he still felt the guilt gripping his heart. Other men had arrived, and they offered to take Mr. Browne away. Wayne released him and approached Lily, but remained two or three steps away. His reluctant wife still crouched beside the wagon wheel, her hands covering her face as sobs wracked her body.

"Lily?" he whispered hoarsely. When she didn't look up and didn't respond, he continued, "I'm so sorry."

She wailed then. The floodgates that she'd been holding back ripped open, and her cries were like those of mourning that he'd never heard before. His own tears streamed down his face. All he wanted to do was hold her and take care of her, but he knew that he couldn't. He couldn't afford for her to get sick. He couldn't afford for her to die. He couldn't afford for them to make Thomas sick so that he too would cause her to mourn this terribly again. No. Wayne would keep his distance, even though it was one of the hardest things he'd ever had to do.

CHAPTER 12

NEAR THE DALLES

When they finally reached Nez Perce, they'd lost three more lives due to the illness—all children—which brought down the morale of the train. They camped at a reasonable distance from the Fort for five more days, until every symptom of the illness had left the camp entirely, then they were finally able to continue their journey.

"We're almost there, aren't we?" Thomas asked from the back of the wagon.

Lily nodded, gripping the mule's reins tighter, thankful to see flatter land, fields of green for the oxen and to be out of the snowy miserable cold of the mountain. She took a deep breath, agreeing that the air seemed lighter and cleaner here than it did back in Virginia, and happy that Thomas already showed so much improvement that he didn't even seem sick any more. She met eyes with him a moment. "Mr. Cooper says we're almost at the Barlow Toll Road, then it's eighty miles... about four or five days before we reach Oregon City."

"Less than a week!" Thomas said with excitement, a small smile tugging his lip. He'd hardly smiled for the past two weeks since they'd had to bury their father.

Honestly, she hadn't smiled either, but seeing Thomas break that ice made her lip tug upward, too. "Less than a week," she confirmed.

Why did that seem like such a long time still? It was barely October. They'd been traveling on this trail for just over five months, but so much had changed. Bingo was no longer tied to the back of her wagon, Lacy was there. Instead, Bingo was tied to the wagon in front of her, a constant, unpleasant reminder that it wasn't her father driving the oxen in the wagon ahead of her, it was Wayne. Her husband.

Her fake husband.

It was the first time in a long time that she'd thought about him as fake since the first week of their marriage. They'd been so awkward then. Over time, they'd become friends—no, great friends—and Lily had come to rely upon him so much that she didn't know how she was going to live without him once they reached Oregon City. So much had changed in the past five months. Her father, who'd been so excited about starting a new life, was gone. Her brother had flourished and bloomed like a flower on the trail and the further they got from the cities and dust and such back east, the better his health seemed to improve, and one would hardly believe he was sick at all if they'd just met him now. And then there was Lily, herself. She'd wanted nothing more than to live in Oregon with her father and brother and to teach and play with children in a school, much like she'd done for most of the trail. But some of those children were gone now, either turned back or buried by their mothers, and Lily's heart broke when she thought about those sweet faces. Things had changed so much. Now she would have to care for her brother without her father's guidance. And Thomas, being more than ten years younger than Lily's twenty, was nearly like having a child of her own.

Could she really teach school and raise Thomas together? Yes, chances were that he'd be attending school with her in one room with the rest of the children in whatever town they settled, but she'd not be able to give him the individual attention that he deserved. She knew children thrived on loving careful upbringing, the way that she had. And the last thing she wanted to do was neglect Thomas.

And then there was Wayne. How did he figure into all of this? What would Wayne want at the end of the journey? The Browne family had asked so much of him. Her father had told her where their money had been hidden in the bottom of the grandfather clock, so that when the time came, they could buy the land they needed to and to pay Wayne the two hundred dollars that he'd promised him. Two hundred dollars used to seem like a lot of money to Lily, but it didn't seem like nearly enough for all that Wayne had done for them. He'd stepped up and been better than a friend, better than any husband that Lily could have imagined for herself. Maybe the man had had a rough past, but whatever had happened to him before they'd met had made him into the gentleman that she had today, and she wouldn't have wanted him any other way.

"Whoa," the call came from the front of the train.

Lily answered and began reining in the mules. It grew darker a little earlier in the evening now, but it was probably still nearly an hour until sunset. To allow her rear end a break from the hard wooden plank on which she sat most of the day, she stood and stretched her back, keeping the reins in one hand. Thomas climbed over the seat from the back of the cart. "Can I help with the mules?"

Frowning down at him she sighed. "I suppose so, but don't exert yourself too much."

"Yes!" he cheered as he scrambled down from the seat.

Lily reached into the back of the cart to grab hold of the hobbles before stepping down to help her brother. Together they released the harnesses and each of them led a mule toward the the oxen at the cart ahead of them. There they met with Wayne who smiled up at them as he unharnessed the last of the oxen. Lily stepped forward to take hold of the lead rope from one ox.

Wayne took hold of the other two, and the three of them led the animals toward the designated grazing area. Once all the animals were hobbled, the threesome headed toward the camp and chuck wagon. It was a great blessing that they had food to spare again and could eat meals together with the whole camp.

Mr. Avery had been highly apologetic the whole way since the sickness they'd carried affected the whole camp. Four lives lost—no, five, including Mr. Avery's own son. He and his family stood in line at the chuck wagon just ahead of Lily, Wayne, and Thomas. One of the mothers who'd lost a daughter spit in his direction and cursed at him as she passed.

In some ways, Lily wanted to join the mother in the hatred that she felt. If it hadn't been for the Avery family, maybe her father would still be alive. But her heart told her that it was just as possible that they wouldn't have found that spring when they did, and it had been days before they'd come to the Fort at Nez Perce where they could have access to a well. They might have all died of dehydration without the Averys' help. Besides, her father would have wanted her to forgive. And how could she accept God's forgiveness for her own sin if she couldn't forgive Mr. Avery?

Everyone got their bowl of stew and chunk of bread and went to sit in the grass near the fire. Wayne spread out a canvas blanket and offered for Lily and Thomas to sit first. Always the gentleman.

"Do you think we can start reading the story again today?" Thomas asked.

Since they'd gone through so much—the bandits, the food shortage, the dehydration, the sickness, and the death of their father—they'd stopped reading *The Count of Monte Cristo,* since they were rarely together as a threesome anymore. But there was a small window of opportunity that Thomas seemed to have noticed when the sun hadn't quite set yet, after dinner, where they were together with enough time to read a chapter or so. But would it be prudent? She cast a questioning glance over toward Wayne.

His eyes were sad but hopeful looking as he nodded.

She didn't realize what a relief it was for her that he wanted to continue the story, too. Even though it had been nearly a month since they'd stopped reading the book together, and there were only a couple chapters to the story left, she too wanted to feel some sort of normalcy again. "All right," she said to Thomas. "After you finish your plate, you can go to the cart and get the book."

"Hurray!" And then Thomas tucked in with greater appetite than Lily had seen in a while, it made her grin to witness it.

When he'd finished, he handed his bowl to Lily and took off toward the cart. "Slow down. Don't exert yourself," she called after him to no avail.

"He's doing much better today than of late," Wayne said before eating a bite of his stew soaked bread. Like Lily, Wayne seemed to hold his bread til the end of the meal and then use it to wipe the bowl clean.

She stacked the bowl her brother gave her under her own. "He does. I'm glad for it."

"It's not long before we reach Oregon, now," he said with a sigh as he finished his last bite.

Lily couldn't help but sigh with him. "Less than a week."

"As soon as we get there, I'll go to the judge and make our annulment official. I don't want for either of us to feel awkward about that situation. I imagine it's better to not waste time about it," he said quietly.

Shock poured over Lily and shook her to the core. The annulment. She'd all but forgotten it. And she certainly didn't expect it to be brought up so soon. Didn't she still have days to decide whether that was what she really wanted? But maybe she was just being selfish. Obviously this was what Wayne wanted, since he could be so cold about it. Maybe all the warmth she'd felt there had been her imagination. She swallowed down the tears that stung the backs of her eyes and nodded. "All right."

"Here," Thomas was back in a flash and shoving the book into Lily's hands.

Lily stared down at it like it was a foreign object

A JOURNEY FOR LILY

for a moment. She didn't want to read it anymore. But Thomas was waiting... cheerfully waiting, and when she glanced up at Wayne, who was smiling and sitting with Thomas on his lap, she knew that she would disappoint him too if she gave into her selfish whim and refused to read. After letting out a slow breath, she opened the book to the marked page and began to read.

WAYNE WAS IN LOVE WITH LILY. HE ADMITTED IT TO himself. He'd never felt more strongly about a woman—no a person—than he did about her. This all came as a surprise to him, but he knew that if he loved her, truly and deeply, that he needed to let her go. She was smarter than him, better than him, and so very pretty. There was no way that he could wish that she would love him in return. After all, she had dreams and aspirations. She wanted to become a schoolteacher. And to do that, she needed to be unwed. He couldn't hang onto her, no matter how much he wanted to.

The Barlow Toll Road was a rough terrain to cross, and Wayne had been helping Mr. Cooper grease the wheels every other day on the wagons to help keep the axles from as much damage as possible as they traversed the land. After only three and a half days, they made it to the Willamette Valley and Oregon City.

They'd finally made it. When he hopped down off the ox cart in front of the land bureau, Wayne wanted to run up to Lily and hug her but refrained. It had been so easy between them while traveling, but ever since he'd distanced himself while sick, they'd never touched like that again, and the friendliness they'd had before slowly faded. Still, he couldn't hold back the wide grin as he approached her cart, patting the mule on the neck as he strode toward them. "We're here."

"We are," her grin was just as wide, and it made his heart swell.

Thomas hopped down too and ran toward him, throwing himself at Wayne and into an embrace. "Wayne, it's amazing. We're here. Oregon"

Wayne huffed a laugh, so happy for the way that Thomas's youth kept him from feeling any of that awkwardness that was between him and Lily. "Oregon," Wayne repeated, feeling like it was unreal. It was midday and they were already finished with their travels.

Thomas pulled back and grabbed a hold of Lily, pulling his sister closer. "Family hug."

And then Thomas's arms were around both Wayne and Lily, pulling them both closer together then they'd been in more than a month. When did it get so difficult for them to be close together? Face flushed, Lily patted Wayne gently on the shoulder and he did the same to her, feeling heat in his own cheeks.

Finally, Thomas released them both and took off toward the back of the cart.

Lily took an uneasy step back, and Wayne did the same, creating that more comfortable distance again. The sun was almost directly overhead. That meant that he had time. He cleared his throat. "I suppose now would be as good a time as any to go over to the judge and make arrangements for that annulment. I could go and do that before supper, even."

Lily's face fell and she cast her glance downward. "I suppose it's necessary," she said, and then she looked up, searching for his gaze. "But, do you feel... I mean do you think—no." She shook her head, then said, "Wait a minute."

After stepping to the back of the ox cart, she pulled herself up to the back and shuffled around in the belongings for a moment before jumping back down with a billfold. Wayne frowned as she approached, looking in the billfold. She removed two crisp hundred dollar bills and then shoved them toward Wayne.

"I believe this is what I owe you for your help."

He frowned, his heart sinking to his stomach. After shoving his hands in his pockets, he shook his head. "You don't owe me anything."

Her brow scrunching over her forehead, she tilted her head in that cute, questioning way that he'd always liked seeing. "But you and father had a deal."

"Yes, that I'd help your family and protect them on the trail. But your father... he didn't make it. So I failed."

Her eyes went wide. "Absolutely not. That wasn't your fault. There was nothing you could do in that situation. You didn't fail."

Tears stung the backs of his eyes and his chest ached more. "But I did. The three of you didn't arrive safely, like I promised. It isn't right for you to pay me. Use that toward your land. That's what would make your father happy."

Her nostrils flared. "My father would want me to pay what I owe you. You can't decline."

A twinge of anger rose up in him at her stubbornness. "But I do decline."

Her hands went to her hips. "I insist that you take the money."

"I insist that you keep it."

"Why do you insist on being so stubborn and heaping guilt upon yourself for things you didn't do? You had nothing to do with my father's death. Nothing to do with Caleb's, either. You can't always take responsibility for when bad things happen."

"But if they are my responsibility, then I can take it."

"But it's not," she said as tears welled in her eyes. She blinked and they slipped down her cheeks. "You're so frustrating and stubborn and kind and dumb!" She yelled.

That last one hurt him to the core. He still struggled with his reading, but he'd gotten so much better. But he guessed if anyone earned the right to call him dumb, it was Lily, since she was the one who'd helped him learn to read.

Tears continued to stream down her face. "Dumb! Why are you talking to me about an annulment, Wayne? A dumb, stupid annulment. Can't you see that I can't live without you? That I'll die if you leave me, Wayne. Can't you see that I love you with all my heart—loved you since before my father died… before you even took me for a ride on Lacy for my birthday. I had already decided in my heart that I didn't want to get a stupid annulment. Why couldn't you see all of that? Why couldn't you love me back?"

Now she was sobbing and had shoved her face in her hands, the two hundred dollar bills still pressed between her thumb and forefinger.

And Wayne just stood there, blinking at her. "You… You love me?"

She didn't look up—she nodded into her hands.

His heart skipped a beat. She loved him. In all his ugliness and stupidity, stubbornness and simplicity, she loved him—even though he wasn't worth the two hundred dollars she held. He gently took hold of her hands and pulled them from her face. She resisted at first but allowed it. Her blue eyes were red-rimmed, and her face was covered in wetness from her tears. But she'd never looked so beautiful. When her eyes finally met his, he said, "Lily, I've loved you since I first saw you, the day before we actually met—the day before we were married. I saw you and you looked at me and smiled and my heart told me that I'd never love a woman more than I loved you. Over the months and miles on the trail, my love for you has grown from a little spark to a roaring flame—a forest fire, even. But I thought I needed to push all of that aside because you could never love me."

Her brow furrowed. "Why would you think that?"

He shook his head and pulled her to him. "It doesn't matter now. It only matters that you do love me. You do, right?'

She nodded against his chest. "I do."

Taking hold of her shoulders he pushed her back enough to see her face again and leaned in. "I do, too."

And then he kissed her gently on the lips, brushing his against hers and then pulled back again. Wayne caressed Lily's delicate face, scarcely believing the miraculous truth—this captivating woman wanted to stay married to him. After so much heartache, fate had granted him more than he ever dreamed.

"Lily..." he whispered reverently, the depth of his love boundless in those two hallowed syllables.

Her glistening eyes answered with wordless longing. Slowly, nervously, he leaned in again. Her sweet breath mingled with his, both suspended in anticipation.

The moment their lips met, rapture jolted

through Wayne's body. Lily's hands reached up around his shoulders and then clung to him tightly, eliminating any remaining distance. Their kiss deepened, communicating all Wayne's unspoken feelings. Her fingers threading through his hair sent shivers racing down his spine.

"Lily?" Thomas called gently from their side. "What's that money for?"

Reluctantly their lips parted, foreheads touching for a brief moment before they both chuckled and pulled back. Then Lily looked down at Thomas and shook her head and then said, "Nothing... Family hug," and pulled Thomas into their embrace.

And this time, Wayne truly felt a part of the family.

EPILOGUE

October 1855

WEST LINN, OREGON

Thomas sighed as he sat in the rough hewn bench of the one room schoolhouse. It had been a year since he, his sister, and Wayne had arrived in Oregon. He'd never realized that school could be such a bore. Long sessions of math, reading, and learning that were dumbed down for the other kids in his grade level. Lily had already taught him all these things over the years of practicing to be a teacher.

That day, she stood in front of the classroom with a hand on the small bump on her belly. The school master had asked if she would teach school for them until they could find a replacement or until she had a baby—one or the other. And the baby was due the beginning of next year. That wasn't much time to find a replacement, Thomas supposed.

"Lunch time," Lily called from the front of the room. And the other children leapt from the chairs grabbing their pails from the back of the classroom and careening outside but Thomas had bad news, so he slowly got up and headed up to his teacher.

"Mrs. Cody," he called her, since they'd discussed how it wasn't appropriate for him to call her Lily in school.

"What is it, Thomas?" she asked, lifting a brow.

He sighed. "I forgot my lunch today."

Her brow furrowed immediately. "Oh... well then you can take mine."

He shook his head. Ever since she'd been with child, she'd been eating the strangest things. The last thing he wanted to find out was that there was chicken or egg in his peanut butter sandwich or something like that.

"Lily!" a voice called from the back of the class-room. Wayne walked toward them in his overalls looking like he'd run the whole way there. He still had a hammer stuck in the loop on his side, since he was a carpenter in town and was working on building a new hospital. "Thomas forgot his lunch this morning. I'm not too late, am I?"

She laughed, her hand fluttering toward her lips. "Nope. You're just in time."

Thomas rolled his eyes as Wayne stepped forward and offered Lily a kiss on the cheek. At least it was on the cheek this time, since usually it was a Kissy-Fest. And he hated when they got like that and needed to leave for another room. Then Lily hugged Wayne, and Thomas knew it was coming. He snatched his lunch pail from Wayne's hand and took off after the other children out in the recess yard. His memories of his mother and father and the affection they had for each other were heartwarming, but for some reason he didn't like to stick around for the affection between those two. Maybe there was a difference between couples who were married for twenty one years and one year. Thomas didn't know...

But he did look forward to getting a little niece or nephew to join him soon so their family could be even more complete. He'd overheard Lily tell Wayne that she wanted to name the baby Cecil if it was a boy and Marie if it was a girl. Thomas approved. They were both his parents' names, and it made him even happier that the baby would get a good, strong name when they were born.

Melody waved at him from a fallen log and said "Thomas! Sit with me."

He shrugged and made his way over, butterflies fluttering in his stomach. He wondered if this was what love felt like. Did Lily and Wayne feel this way about each other? He shook his head. No matter. It was going to be a long, long, long time before he initiated a Kissy-fest with anyone.

THE END

ABOUT THE SERIES

Ready for the next book? Don't miss the rest of the
RELUCTANT WAGON TRAIN BRIDE SERIES!

*"The west is too wild for an unwed woman. If you want
to ride on my wagon train and make it to Oregon, you'll
need to find yourself a husband."*

THE RELUCTANT WAGON TRAIN BRIDE ~

Twenty brides find themselves in a compromising situation – they have to get married in order to travel to Oregon on their wagon train. Every story in the series is a clean, standalone romance. Will the bride end up falling in love with their reluctant husband? Or will they get an annulment when they reach Oregon? Each bride has a different story ~ Read all of them and don't miss out!

RELUCTANT WAGON TRAIN BRIDE SERIES!

ABOUT THE AUTHOR

P. Creeden is the sweet romance and mystery pen name for USA Today Bestselling Author, Pauline Creeden. Her stories feature down-to-earth characters who often feel like they are undeserving of love for one reason or another and are surprised when love finds them.

Animals are the supporting characters of many of her stories, because they occupy her daily life on the farm, too. From dogs, cats, and goldfish to horses, chickens, and geckos -- she believes life around pets is so much better, even if they are fictional. P. Creeden married her college sweetheart, who she also met at a horse farm. Together they raise a menagerie of animals and their one son, an avid reader, himself.

If you enjoyed this story, look forward to more books by P. Creeden.
In 2024, she plans to release more than 12 new books!
Hear about her newest release, FREE books when they come available, and giveaways hosted by the author—subscribe to her newsletter:
https://www.subscribepage.com/pcreedenbooks

Join the My Beta and ARC reader Group on Facebook!
I publish a new story every other month on average!

If you enjoyed this book and want to help the author, consider leaving a review at your favorite book seller – or tell someone about it on social media. Authors live by word of mouth!

LOVE WESTERN ROMANCE?

Join the Historical Western Romance Readers on Facebook to hear about more great books, play fun games, and often win prizes!

Dorothy Mason swore that she'd never marry again when her husband passed away five years ago. She just wasn't interested in her heart being broken again. But living in her old house in Tennessee kept breaking it by reminding her daily of her times with her husband, and she was having a difficult time letting go. So, her sister convinces her to get a fresh start by traveling west on the wagon train to Oregon. But once she's given up her life and everything dear to her and arrives in Missouri, Dorothy discovers that she can't move forward unless she considers getting married again.

Reverend Elias Stone doesn't quite believe in Manifest Destiny, but does believe in bringing lost souls to the Lord. With so many lost people moving out west in search of gold and riches, Elias feels a calling on his life to make a move in that direction, himself. So, he arranges to join a wagon train heading to Oregon and California. But before the journey even starts, he finds himself in a harrowing situation that could take his life, calling, and ability to travel away from him. Only by considering a marriage to a woman he doesn't even know can he continue, but is this really God's plan for him?

Get your copy of A Journey for Dorothy!

And check out the rest of the books in The Reluctant Wagon Train Bride Series:

"The west is too wild for an unwed woman. If you want to ride on my wagon train and make it to Oregon, you'll need to find yourself a husband."

THE RELUCTANT WAGON TRAIN BRIDE ~ Twenty brides find themselves in a compromising situation. They have to get married in order to travel to Oregon on their wagon train. Each story in the series is a clean, standalone romance. Will the bride end up falling in love with her reluctant husband? Or will she get an annulment when they reach Oregon? Each bride has a different story ~ Read each one and don't miss out!

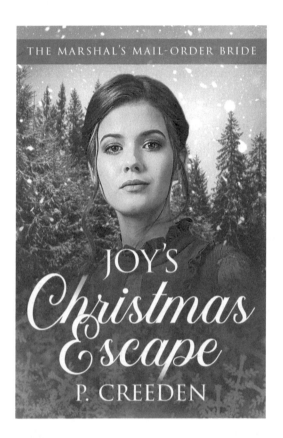

With danger and redemption swirling around them, can an unlikely Christmas miracle still be found in Carson City?

Schoolteacher Joy Stewart has never been lucky. Her father died before she was born. Her mother left her in the care of her grandmother so that she could get remarried and move far away. So when her grandmother succumbs to illness, her debtors come to call. And one of them has his eyes set on Joy to be his bride as payment for his debt. That bad luck just seems to be compounding on Joy—what she needs is a Christmas Miracle, and her grandmother has put a plan in the works…

Marshal Jack Bolling has found himself in want of a nanny. With the death of his sister and her husband in a tragic accident, he has now come into possession of his twin niece and nephew of four years old. For over a month he's had no luck in locating an appropriate nanny for them—at least not on his salary and what a marshal can afford. But then his good friend, Pastor North has the idea that perhaps Jack should be looking for a wife instead? The thought of that sends chills down Jack's spine, but when he ends up putting the twins' lives in danger due to his job, he wonders what choice he has. But can he even dare to hope that he'd be lucky enough to find a wife so close to Christmastime?

Get your copy of Joy's Christmas Escape!

And check out the rest of the books in The Marshal's Mail-Order Bride series:

THE MARSHAL'S MAIL ORDER BRIDE ~ Eight brides each find themselves in a compromising situation – and the only way out is to escape west and become a mail-order bride. But will trouble follow them? Good thing they are heading into the arms of a law man. Each bride has a different, stand alone story ~ Read each one and don't miss out!

Made in United States
Troutdale, OR
09/28/2024

23187707R00106